MURDER AT THE PIER

A Sister Sleuths Mystery
Book 1

RAYNA MORGAN

Copyright Notice

Contents

Chapter One

Lea and the dogs started the day in the doghouse. The only way to get out was to promise Paul that their sleuthing escapades were over. But could she keep that promise?

The answer came that night in the form of the dead body the dogs found under the Pier.

* * *

Paul walked into the kitchen. The border collie crept into a corner, covering her right eye with a paw.

"You're not the only one who should be hiding this morning," he scolded.

"Surely you aren't referring to me," Lea laughed, following her husband into the kitchen. Trailing her hand across his shoulders, she reached behind him for the coffee pot.

"It's hard to be upset with this little dog," he mumbled, looking down at the sleek body of gold and white fur, steely black eyes, and pointed ears. He turned back to his wife. "You and your sister are another story. You could have gotten yourselves or this dog hurt last night."

Lea filled her husband's coffee mug. "At least we discovered the source of the ghosts in Mrs. Allen's house."

"I'm sure our neighbor will be eternally grateful," he scoffed, "but you two agreeing to stake out her back yard all night could have resulted in consequences you didn't plan on."

"But it didn't. And I learned something from our efforts."

"What would that be?"

"Intruders come in all shapes and sizes."

"Thanks to you, I'm sure our neighbor will sleep much better tonight. Living alone makes her nervous enough without being spooked by noises at night. But since you and your sister have taken up this new interest in sleuthing, my sleeping habits haven't improved." He added cream to his coffee. "With Mrs. Allen's penchant for gossip, the entire neighborhood will hear about your detecting skills. You'll be famous or should I say infamous?"

"Just be thankful I didn't have Spirit with us." Lea glanced at the white golden retriever lounging on the patio. "At least Gracie had the sense not to attack the skunk. Spirit would have tried to play with the intruder and been sprayed from head to foot."

"You mean because Spirit thinks every person and every animal he encounters is friendly and wants to play?"

"Exactly why we didn't take him. His investigative skills are a little lacking, and I don't think the breed name is even applicable in his case. Spirit couldn't retrieve his own shadow following him."

"It's alright, boy, your sweetness more than makes up." Paul scratched the long, floppy ears of the dog that had entered the kitchen upon hearing his name.

Lea's lower lip protruded in a pout. "I'll admit we probably only got rid of Mrs. Allen's culprit because he was more afraid of Gracie than she was of him."

"It hardly ranks you and Maddy with Sherlock and the other great detectives."

Hearing his name, the black and gray striped cat twisted his neck. "He's not talking about you, Sherlock. Go back to sleep," Lea laughed.

"So maybe we'll have a little peace and quiet tonight?"

"You have nothing to worry about," Lea assured her husband. "Maddy and I have limited our sleuthing to four-legged intruders."

"Let's keep it that way," Paul suggested.

"Anything special on your agenda today?"

"I'm meeting with a client this afternoon about the recent burglaries at construction sites. He wants to know what security measures he should take so his sites don't get hit."

Paul's consulting business included advising clients on all aspects of commercial real estate including development, leasing, and management. Security and related staffing issues fell under the venue of site maintenance.

Lea frowned. "I saw it on the news. The press has dubbed them the Construction Site Burglars. It's a bad business alright. What did the reporter say, five places hit already? It's fortunate nobody's been hurt."

Paul nodded. "The reason my client is worried. He's not only afraid of losing a lot of valuable equipment but of putting his security personnel in harm's way trying to protect his properties."

Lea leaned over to stroke Gracie's head. "What are you recommending?"

"A number of things can be done. I'm doing a physical inspection of his sites this morning to see what's lacking. In fact, I better get a move on if I want to visit all of them before I meet with him later today."

"I hope for your client's sake the police catch the culprits soon." She added an afterthought: "Be sure to let him know if he needs an employee safety manual, I'm available to produce one."

As a freelance business writer, Lea prepared employee handbooks, marketing brochures, proposals, and shareholder reports for her clients. She also wrote speeches and advertising copy as needed.

"Don't worry. I plug my brilliant wife's skills at every opportunity." He flashed the smile that still melted Lea's heart after so many years of marriage.

"Will Tom be coming over after the game?" she asked.

Their close friend, Tom Elliot, head of the Major Crime Detective Unit of the Buena Viaje Police Department, had earned his reputation as a smart, conscientious, hard-working officer; respected and well-liked by the men and women he supervised.

Lea was referring to their Monday night routine of Tom joining them for dinner after Paul and Tom played softball with the local league. Divorced, Tom always welcomed a respite from frozen or fast food, his typical fare.

"I don't know if he'll make the game. He's had his hands full with the burglaries the last couple of days. From what he told me yesterday, they're no closer to catching the perpetrators."

"I'd never think of a construction site being the location of a crime. What's Tom told you about the burglaries?" Lea inquired, trying to show as little interest as possible.

"According to him, construction site burglary is a growing problem." Paul stuffed papers into his briefcase. "Offenders have different motivations. Amateurs take building materials for use in their own houses: plywood, pavers, or ladders. Professional thieves take property they can sell in an unregulated second-hand market: appliances, doors, and windows. Insiders may be more likely to take heavy equipment which takes more skill or effort to remove."

"What's the extent of losses in these burglaries?"

"Apparently billions of dollars worth of materials and equipment are stolen every year. Indirect expenses include job delays and higher insurance premiums. Unfortunately, those losses are passed on to home buyers, resulting in increased prices."

"I can understand why they've got every available officer working the case but if Tom has to work tonight and can't make the game," she mocked, "won't it be a little hard for your team to win without the star hitter?"

Paul winced, grabbing his sunglasses and heading for the door. "I'll do my best to cover the gap."

He yelled up the stairs. "I'm leaving if you want a ride to school, Jon."

4

"Two minutes, Dad."

Handing Paul the car keys he was looking for, Lea said: "If Tom comes for dinner, he can give us the latest news on the burglaries."

"Don't even think about it, Lea. Even though you and your sister . . . and your dogs," he added, looking directly at the canines, "love to play at sleuthing, you can all keep your noses out of this one. It's too dangerous. The biggest concern of the police right now is the perpetrators seem to be getting more aggressive with each incident. No one's been hurt yet and no weapons have been used, but the police are afraid that will be the next step since most of the owners of construction sites, including my clients, have beefed up their security."

"Don't worry," she assured him, tossing her long, copper-colored hair. "I've got enough on my plate right now to keep me plenty busy. I have no time for distractions."

She watched their tall, gangly son come running down the stairs, backpack bouncing. A freshman in high school, he was experiencing such a growth spurt she hardly knew who would emerge from his bedroom each morning. He grabbed the toast she had ready giving her a quick peck on the cheek. "Thanks, Mom. See you later."

"Have a good day, you two." Lea answered her buzzing cell phone, waving Paul and Jon out the door.

"Hey, Sis, hope you were up."

"Of course. Enjoying my second cup of coffee with the dogs before I start work."

Getting a call from Maddy this early in the day was unusual. "Are you at the furniture store already?"

Her sister worked as an interior design consultant and salesperson at one of the local furniture stores.

"No, I'm off today. I switched shifts with one of the other salespeople who had a wedding to attend." Maddy's voice raised an octave. "But we've already had some excitement around here."

5

Lea perked up. "What's going on?"

"Have you heard about the Construction Site Burglars?"

"Paul and I were just discussing them. He's gone to a meeting with a client concerned enough with the burglaries to implement additional security measures. Where did you hear about them?"

"I stopped by Starbucks for a cup of coffee. The regular coffee clutch was nattering full speed with news of last night's break-in."

Lea gasped. "It didn't happen in your neighborhood, did it? It would be a new modus operandi if the burglary was carried out in an area where people are living."

"No, but it was right up the street at the site where they're building those condominiums . . . the project called Two Palms. Come on over; I'll tell you all about it. We could even go see where it happened," Maddy tempted, knowing Lea wouldn't be able to resist.

Lea was the more reserved of the two sisters, the one who planned ahead and thought things through. Maddy was impulsive, spontaneous. She was also irresistible, with her exuberant personality. Ever since childhood, she had been able to talk her younger sister into any new adventure.

In spite of the pile of work sitting on her desk, Lea's hesitation was brief. "Give me twenty minutes."

Grabbing her purse as she headed for the back door, she called to Gracie: "Let's go, girl. Paul wouldn't be happy if he knew, but all we're going to do is take a look."

* * *

The familiar drive to Maddy's was one of her favorites because it gave her a view of the ocean. Not a day passed without Lea admiring the small coastal town where they lived, bounded by houses climbing up the hill on one side and the Pacific Ocean on the other.

When she and Paul moved to Buena Viaje to be closer to Paul's aging parents, they appreciated the fact that although the town itself was small, access to a major metropolitan area was within an hour's drive. Initially, Lea commuted on crowded freeways to get to the corporate offices where she was employed. Now she worked from home and days of facing bumper to bumper traffic were a thing of the past.

It was hard for her to believe how the countryside had changed as she observed more agricultural land being readied for construction.

For years, much of the acreage surrounding the city had been planted in citrus trees. Many of the landowners participated in a preservation program which required retaining the land in agriculture in exchange for a reduction in property taxes. In recent years, those contracts had been expiring. More and more of the land was being sold to developers anxious to build homes and shopping centers for a populace willing to endure longer and longer commutes into the crowded metropolis in order to provide their families with a healthier, more relaxed living environment.

Exiting the freeway and turning onto the two-lane street leading to Maddy's neighborhood, Lea observed the Two Palms project being built on a parcel previously covered with orange trees. The day the builder had ordered the heavy machinery crews to tear out the citrus trees, Maddy and Lea had watched from the corner restaurant, sipping wine and lamenting the loss of more undeveloped land.

As she drove past, she saw a police car and other vehicles including a local news van parked at the site. Several people were milling around including someone holding a large video camera propped on his shoulder. A reporter was holding a microphone in front of a man Lea recognized to be the local Chief of Police.

7

Lea hoped Maddy's coffee klatch would have answers to the questions the Police Chief was being asked.

Chapter Two

Seagate, the small residential area where Maddy lived, was built on what was formerly marshland between the Pier and the Harbor. The state-owned Seagate Beach didn't get as many tourists as beaches near the downtown area.

The neighborhood was originally a hodge-podge of rental dwellings, weekend cottages, and vacant lots. Over years of successive real estate booms, it became a fashionable but eclectic mix of newer homes and older beach cottages. The previous lack of building restrictions had left Seagate with widely varying architectural styles and a spotty retail area.

There were several restaurants a short walk from Maddy's house but they were subject to seasonal fluctuations. The smaller ones unable to sustain enough business during the winter months went out of business.

There wasn't much traffic in the area, but the streets were narrow making parking difficult. Her sister's cottage was on one of the lanes leading directly to the beach.

Turning into the second driveway on Fuchsia Lane, Lea saw her sister pruning rose bushes in her front yard. The sun reflected off the honey blond highlights in the woman's long brown hair.

"Your flowers are stupendous," Lea noted, lowering the tailgate for Gracie. "I'm envious." Her sister had inherited an undeniable green thumb, as well as dazzling hazel eyes, from their father.

Maddy turned to embrace the dog. "Hey, Gracie. How's our partner in crime, or should I say crime prevention? Have you recovered from our little adventure last night?"

The dog wagged her tail eagerly in response. Leading the way inside, the border collie began searching for the tennis ball Maddy typically hid for her. She checked eagerly in all the suspect places: behind the potted plant, under the rug, between the floor pillows.

Setting a water bowl on the floor, Maddy laughed. "You'll have to work harder than that this time."

Gracie happily accepted the challenge, pursuing it doggedly while Maddy turned her conversation to Lea.

"So here's the latest gossip. The couple who live at the entrance to the neighborhood heard noise at the construction site last night around midnight. Typically, the Johnstons, along with the rest of us, would have been sound asleep by midnight. We're all early to bed, early to rise here," Maddy noted, filling ice tea glasses as she continued. "When Mr. Johnston walked outside and looked in the direction of the noise, he saw flashlights toward the back of the site and heard a man shouting. There was no sign of the security guard who's usually in the construction trailer parked at the front. Deciding to err on the side of caution, he called the police and reported a possible burglary in progress."

"That was intuitive. I would have made the mistake of thinking the activity was a delivery of materials to the site or there was some other plausible explanation."

"Me, too, except for the lateness of the hour. When the police arrived, they found the security guard on the floor of the trailer, wrists and ankles bound with masking tape. There were obvious signs of a break-in but no sign of the burglars."

Lea's eyes widened. "How much did they get?"

"We won't know until we hear the news report but from the amount of activity there all morning, the loss must have been significant."

Lea glanced at Gracie, ears pointed, listening intently to Maddy's narration as she chewed on a slobbery tennis ball. "I see you discovered the hiding place, girl. Obviously not as difficult to find as Maddy thought it would be."

"It's her natural sleuthing skills. Between her nose and her instincts, she always finds what she's after. Too bad the police can't use her to catch those burglars."

"I wish we could find out more. I'm sure the police are keeping any outsiders away for now," Lea added, disappointed.

"Probably, but I've got a better idea." Maddy's eyes sparkled. "Let's go see Maria at the donut shop. She knows everything that goes on around here. If there's any new information, you can count on Maria to know what it is."

"Good idea. We'll meet you there." Gracie jumped up, excited to be included in another escapade.

* * *

Lea drove through Seagate to the strip shopping center behind the gas station on the corner. Maria's Donut Shop was between the bank and the convenience store at the end of the center. It was a small store with four wooden tables inside and two tables with umbrellas in front.

Parking her car, Lea realized how fortuitous their timing had been. When they passed the construction site, the news van was nowhere in sight. Now, here it was, in front of Maria's.

Lea stopped Gracie at the front door of the store. "Stay, Gracie. Good girl."

Hearing the shop keeper's bell when Lea and Maddy walked in, Maria waved hello but kept talking rapidly in Spanish to a man wearing a black shirt with the letters KDHY. The only other customer was sitting alone at one of the tables near the front window.

Lea and Maddy made small talk while the men at the counter selected their donuts and finished their conversation with Maria. When one of them stopped to pet Gracie on their way out, Lea smiled innocently: "Busy day already?"

11

"Stocking up on Maria's chocolate glazed donuts," he smiled, departing quickly.

"They play it close to the vest," Lea observed as they approached Maria.

Maddy queried Maria, pulling no punches: "Were they here to do a story on the condo site burglary?"

"Oh, sure," Maria exclaimed, her arms waving in her animated style of conversing.

Maddy always marveled that Maria was so petite considering she was surrounded by yummy donuts and other bakery items every day. Her three young children who helped her when they weren't in school were all of the same petite build.

"The man I was talking to is my cousin. He's the one who carries the television camera when they're interviewing someone," she explained proudly.

Lea pointed to several of the crullers in the glass display case as Maria continued, bagging Lea's pastries as she talked. "In the interview my cousin recorded, the police admitted they are stymied with these burglaries. They have no leads as to who is doing this bad thing. In the story airing tonight, the Chief will be asking the public to report any suspicious activity."

Lea reached over the counter to pay Maria. "Did you have any new customers in the last couple of days you haven't seen before?"

Maria shook her head adamantly, lapsing partially into her native language: "No, señora. Only my regular customers. Believe me, if I would have seen any suspicious hombres, I would have told my cousin. I don't want any bad men anywhere near my niños."

"I figure it must have been someone with an inside connection to the builder," piped in the other customer, twirling the coffee mug in his hands. All three of them turned to the speaker, easily recognizable as a local rancher from his sunburned face, boots, and black Stetson hat.

Maria walked over to his table to refill his coffee cup. "What do you know, Scott?"

The sisters gave the subject a quick visual. His thick, brown hair was tousled under his hat. His face was strong and defined, his features molded from granite. He had dark eyebrows which sloped downward in a serious expression over brown eyes.

"I know no truck could have driven onto the property without passing the security guard at the front." He stirred sugar into his coffee. "When pieces of the land came out of agricultural preserve, I sold a parcel to the developer building those condos. I know the land like the back of my hand. It's bounded on one side by a ditch you couldn't drive a truck over, and on the other side by a stone wall I built during the rainy season to keep flood waters from destroying my orange trees. The front is secured by wire fencing and the construction trailer where the guard stays during his shift."

"Isn't there a recycle yard at the back of the property?" Maddy asked. "Couldn't someone cross it and get onto the construction site?"

"No way. I know the fellow who owns the yard. He keeps four Rottweilers on the property specifically for that purpose . . . to make sure no one breaks in. If someone had been dumb enough to try to cross his property, the barking would have alerted the security guard and any neighbors for a mile in every direction."

Lea squinted. "Are you suggesting the security guard let the van in?"

"I know the retired cop who's working security there to supplement his pension. He's an honest guy. I'm not suggesting that at all."

"Then what leads you to the conclusion it was somehow an inside job?" Maddy persisted.

"The only way someone could get in was by knowing the exact routine of the security guard. He walks the perimeter of the property at scheduled times. I can tell you from all the days I walked that dirt when I was growing oranges there, it's a good mile to the back of the property. Walking slowly enough to inspect everything as he went, the security guard would be away from his post for more than twenty minutes during any one of those patrols. More than enough time for someone to cut through the front gate and lay in wait to overpower him when he returned. From what I heard your cousin telling you, Maria, it sounds like that's what happened. The perps overcame the guard, drove in, and helped themselves to the goods."

"I didn't hear you telling the police when they stopped in earlier asking questions," Maria scoffed.

Scott shook his head. "Not my job. It's what they're paid for. With our tax money, I might add. Besides, I'm not going to make accusations about any of the builders in the County. I've still got land in agricultural reserve I'm going to want to sell someday."

Hearing a low growl emanating from Gracie, Lea looked toward her dog in surprise. Two Hispanic men climbed down from the cab of a large truck pulled into one of the pumps at the gas station. As one man took care of the fueling, the other walked toward the donut shop. He wore black jeans and a black t-shirt, a knit cap on his head, and a red and black bandana around his neck. He had a stocky build, tattoos on both arms, and walked with an imposing swagger.

Maria's greeting was brief and to the point, totally unlike the wide smile and chattiness she offered most customers. "What will it be this morning, Miguel?"

"Same as always, Maria, and put in an extra chocolate cake donut. I had a rough night. I need a sugar spike." He smiled, but his smile was sneering like he was laughing at an inside joke.

Putting a hand on Gracie's head to calm her, Lea could feel a vibrating growl emanating from deep in the dog's chest.

Maria didn't miss Gracie's reaction. "Hey, girl, I haven't given you a treat yet today."

14

She reached into a tray marked 'For Dogs Only' and picked up a large biscuit in the shape of a bone. Sweeping around the counter, she moved quickly to where Gracie sat, body alert, eyes fixed intently on Miguel. Offering the biscuit with one hand, Maria rubbed the border collie's head with the other.

Dropping money on the counter, Miguel grabbed the bag Maria had placed near the cash register and turned to walk out. As he brushed past Gracie, he glared at the dog with a look that caused the hair on the back of Lea's neck to stand on end.

The silence in the donut shop after he left was palpable.

"Who was he, Maria?" Lea asked, shakily.

"One of the three Ramirez brothers. The mother, she got sick and died a couple of years ago. The father, he left them when the last baby was born. Boys have pretty much grown up on their own. They've been in and out of trouble over the years. The oldest one, Roberto, landed in jail. He was in my store last week telling me he just got released on parole."

Measuring coffee into the brewer, Maria continued: "When they're not getting in trouble, they work construction. In fact, they're working on the site that got robbed last night. Been stopping in every morning when they come to fuel the company trucks."

"Sounds like they've had it pretty rough," Maddy sympathized.

"Yeah, you might feel sorry for them except for their attitude. They're mean. And they're rude. They all got bad manners. Not one of them shows any respect for their elders. Mark my words; no good is going to come from any of those boys," she predicted. "I won't miss having them as customers when they move on to another job."

Turning her attention toward Gracie, Lea could see the dog had relaxed since Miguel had left the premises. "He certainly got your hackles up, didn't he, girl?"

15

Throwing a couple of dollars on the table, the rancher gave Lea some advice. "Dogs are smarter than people about a lot of things, especially when it comes to sorting out the good apples from the rotten ones. Pay attention to what your dog is telling you."

Tipping his hat toward Maddy, the rancher walked out. The color rushed to Maddy's cheeks.

She turned back to reassure Maria. "Don't worry; our police department is efficient. I'm sure they'll bring this whole sorry business to an end soon."

Locking her arm in Lea's as they left the donut shop, Maddy suggested: "And maybe we can help them do exactly that."

* * *

Lea got home in time to put finishing touches on a proposal for a prospective new client and answer her emails before fixing dinner. When her son called to ask if he could stay at his friend's house to eat and study, Lea agreed, reminding him it was his night to take the trash out. "Be sure to do it first thing when you get home so your dad doesn't have to tell you. And don't forget to thank Michael's mother."

Taking a peek at the large roast cooking, Lea called Paul. She caught him on his way to the softball game. "Is Tom going to make it for dinner? If not, we're going to have a lot of leftovers. Jon's eating with the Thompsons tonight."

"As a matter of fact, I just got off the phone with Tom. Since we're playing the early game, he won't be able to break away from the station in time. He'll try to come for dinner about seven-thirty but no guarantees. I should be home and cleaned up by then."

Lea pulled vegetables from the bin to clean. "Glad to hear it. I don't think he's getting many home cooked meals since he and Linda have gone their separate ways."

"I'm sure he misses Linda's gourmet cooking but from the way he talks, it's all he misses of their relationship."

"Men," she scoffed. "See you soon. Good luck with your game."

After feeding the animals, Lea walked into the living room in time to watch the early edition of the news. The Police Chief, dressed in the freshly starched uniform she had seen him in that morning, made his appeal to the public.

"Please keep your eyes open around any construction sites, either residential or commercial. Report any suspicious activity."

"Are certain sites more likely to be hit?" the reporter asked.

"Single family houses, especially those which are somewhat isolated, make good targets because there's less chance of neighbors or passersby seeing or hearing a burglar. Any properties without fencing are asking for trouble. Appliances delivered to a site before locking doors and windows are installed present a timing opportunity savvy burglars watch for."

"If someone sees something suspicious, how should they react?"

"In no instance should you approach anyone you believe is engaged in illegal activity. We've been fortunate so far no one has been hurt, but these things have a nasty way of escalating. Make the right move and call for help if you see anything or anyone you believe is out of place in your neighborhood."

Lea sighed. "If the Chief has been effective in asking the public for help, Tom will be plenty busy. We won't be seeing him for dinner, and we'll be eating leftovers tomorrow night."

Chapter Three

Lea was right in her prediction of her and Paul eating alone. She was wrapping up leftovers when her cell phone rang.

"Hope I'm not disturbing you," Mrs. Allen began.

Calls from Mrs. Allen are almost always disturbing.

"Not at all. I hope you're not having more intruders."

"No; thanks to you, my house is quiet but after all the trouble I put you through last night, I'm calling because I don't want to be an alarmist. I'd like to run something by you before calling the police."

Interest piqued, Lea walked out to the back yard so Paul couldn't overhear. "What's going on?"

"I was at the grocery store and decided to take a little drive around the neighborhood on the way home."

She doesn't have the reputation as the neighborhood busybody for no reason.

"I was close to where they're building the two-story Spanish Colonial by the pond. Do you know the house? Red roof tiles and a turret."

"Unfortunately, I know it only too well. Our snoopy cat Sherlock has been there several times in the last couple of weeks. He seems to like foraging in the tiles and drywall on the site. He also loves high places. Since they haven't installed any windows or doors in the house yet, he's been able to climb all the way to the turret to check out the view. I saw him sitting up there a couple of days ago when I took the dogs for a walk."

"I was a block away from it when I saw lights inside the house. Like flashlight beams," she clarified, "in an upstairs room. Neither the builder nor the owner would be there this time of night. I wouldn't have thought much about it except for the recent news reports on the burglaries."

18

"Did you call the police?"

"No, I was afraid I was overreacting and shouldn't waste their time."

"I don't think that would be the case. I saw the Police Chief interviewed on the news tonight encouraging people to call in any suspicious activity they see. From his description of likely targets, that house might be prone to a break-in."

"There's no fencing around the property," Mrs. Allen agreed, "which would allow for easy access."

"Tell you what. I was getting ready to take Gracie and Spirit for their evening stroll. We'll go for a ride instead and see if there appears to be anything going on."

"Don't put yourself at risk," her neighbor warned.

"Don't worry. We'll keep our distance. The dogs will detect scents from quite a ways off and alert me. If they seem to be reacting, I'll call it in. You won't have to worry about sending up a false alarm."

"Thank you, Lea. Call and let me know what you find to put my mind at ease before I turn in."

"No problem. I'll get my super sleuths right on it," Lea laughed, ringing off.

She walked into the living room where Paul was watching a basketball game. She explained where she was going as she put halters on the dogs. Without taking his eyes off the television screen, Paul asked: "Don't you think you've wasted enough time playing detective for Mrs. Allen?"

"We won't get any closer than a block away. Besides, she's probably overreacting like everyone else in town right now. These burglaries have everyone on edge. I'll call you as soon as we head back home," she assured him.

Jon came through the front door in time to see his mother getting the dogs ready to go somewhere. "Wherever you're off to, can I go? I finished my homework at Michael's house."

19

"Not this time." Without disclosing any concern about possible danger, Lea offered a distraction to discourage her son from joining them. "Your dad's making popcorn at half-time if you want to watch the rest of the game."

"Sounds good." Jon licked his lips and patted his stomach.

By the time Lea got the dogs into the car, Paul and Jon were hollering at the screen, Paul's concern for his wife's safety all but forgotten

* * *

Lea wondered if Paul was right. Was she going against her better judgment driving to the site? At least there was an empty field between the house and the end of the street allowing them to keep their distance.

Nevertheless, getting out of the car at the corner to get a better view, her heart skipped a beat. Mrs. Allen was right: there were lights in the house. A black van was parked in the driveway with the loading doors open. Her neighbor was right about something else: it wouldn't be the owners of the house visiting at this time of night in the dark.

"Hurry up, Miguel," a voice hollered. "We're done here. We'll be late for the meet."

"Come on guys, we're out of here, too," Lea summoned the dogs. Hearing the urgency in his master's voice, Spirit stopped rooted to the spot, but Gracie's instincts kicked in. She went racing toward the site, barking loudly.

The commotion aroused an instantaneous reaction. Two hooded figures came running out of the house, glancing frantically in all directions before racing to the van. Not bothering to secure the back doors, one jumped in the driver's seat and revved the engine while the other jumped into the passenger side.

"No, Spirit," Lea yelled, seeing Spirit join his sister racing for the back of the van. "Come back, Gracie."

20

The retriever hesitated between seeing the back doors of the van flying open in front of him and hearing his master's voice. But the strength of the border collie's hind legs propelled her easily into the back of the van as the vehicle leaped to life weaving crazily down the street. The last thing Lea saw as the van swerved around the corner was Gracie struggling to keep her balance in the back of the careening vehicle.

"Come, Spirit, now," she yelled with authority, sliding behind the wheel of her car and simultaneously opening the other door. The dog jumped into the car and Lea took off in pursuit, hitting the speed dial button on her phone.

"Paul, call Tom at the station right away. Something terrible has happened." They were in a residential neighborhood but Lea was driving as fast as she dared in pursuit of the speeding van. "As Mrs. Allen feared, there was a burglary in progress at the house. Two men stormed out when Gracie ran over barking and took off. They were in such a hurry, they didn't close the back doors of their van and she jumped into it."

"Oh, no," Paul moaned. "Don't tell me you're chasing them."

"What choice do I have? I've got to get off the phone. Call Tom right away. Tell him it's a late model, black, Nissan van headed toward the Pier on Beach Boulevard. I'll call back when I can."

Paul's hands fumbled on the keypad as he dialed Tom's direct line at the police station.

"Tom Elliot," he heard the voice say, glad it wasn't a recording. "How may I be of assistance?"

"Thank goodness, it's you and not your voice mail." He quickly explained the situation exactly as Lea had related it.

"Okay, Paul." Tom switched into the reassuring mode he adopted when handling people in desperate situations. "We're on it. I'll take another squad car with me. Don't worry; we'll find them. The van is probably headed for one of the freeway on-ramps to

21

get out of the area as fast as they can. I'll alert highway patrol units all along the highway. They won't get far."

"Thanks, Tom. Please have Lea call as soon as you've located them."

"Of course," the Detective replied, cutting the call off and putting his game plan into action. Grabbing his jacket, he ran toward the parking lot.

* * *

As Lea waited impatiently for the street light to turn green, she thought how grateful she was Jon hadn't come with her. *I could use another set of eyes to keep the van in sight, but this is hardly the kind of adventure I want my son to be part of.*

The moment the light turned, Lea flattened the gas pedal, throwing Spirit back against the seat. "Sorry, big guy, but I don't have time to stop to put your seat belt on."

Spirit dug his claws into the car seat and held on for dear life, all the time staring straight ahead in the direction where Gracie had gone.

If I'm right about these guys wanting to get out of Buena Viaje as fast as possible, there's only one route that will give them access to the freeway headed north. Under the overpass to the frontage road running parallel to Main Street.

"They'll have four or five stop lights before they hit the freeway," Lea reasoned aloud. "If Tom got Paul's call about my needing help, he'll be thinking the same thing. Hopefully, he's already on his way to intercept them."

Spirit cocked his head listening attentively without averting his eyes from the road.

The fact there were few cars on the street was to Lea's advantage. *Thank heavens, Buena Viaje is usually wrapped up tight by ten o'clock at night.*

22

But just as she sensed she might be closing the gap, a motorcycle roared around her, forcing her to jam on the brakes as the light turned red. Lea's hands were sweating as she gripped the wheel. *Come on, come on, come on.* Time seemed to be standing still and the van was nowhere in sight.

Gunning the engine again before the light changed, her heart dropped as she realized how close they were to the Pier and the last intersection before the freeway access.

"I'm afraid we've lost them, Spirit. I guess I was wrong in my theory about their escape route."

She rounded the curve and drove toward the parking lot at the Pier. That's when she saw it. The lights shone on a single vehicle in the otherwise empty lot: the black van parked at a hasty angle. She swerved the car into the lot so fast Spirit was pitched across the seat, landing against the door.

Lea was so happy to see the van she lost all sense of caution. Almost before the car had rolled to a complete stop, she jumped out leaving Spirit behind barking anxiously. Approaching what appeared to be an empty vehicle, she could see the front doors were wide open leaving the interior lights on. There was no one inside.

The back doors were closed. She walked toward them with great apprehension until she heard the familiar sound of Gracie's barking. Throwing the doors open, she suddenly found herself on the pavement with seventy pounds of dog on top of her, licking her face.

"Okay, girl, you're safe now," she laughed, throwing her arms around the dog. "Thank goodness, you're safe. Let's go get your brother before he breaks through the car window."

With Spirit circling Gracie licking her mouth to show her how happy he was to see her, Lea reached for her phone. In the middle of telling a greatly relieved Paul that she found Gracie and would be heading home, she heard a cacophony of dog wailing coming from under the Pier. Heading toward the noise, Lea expressed exasperation: "I'm ending the call, babe. The dogs are raising a ruckus over something. Let me round them up so I can get out of here."

Lea walked along the Promenade leading to the old wooden structure. The Pier was a favorite attraction for fishing, picnics, and views of the coastline and Islands, but she was in no mood to enjoy the view. She felt impatient crossing the beach as her shoes began filling with sand, certain the dogs had found a dead seagull or leftover hot dog to scuffle over.

Discovering the cause of their agitation, she wasted no time punching Tom's number in her cell phone.

"Where the heck are you, Lea? We've been up and down the frontage road. No sign of the van."

"I found the van abandoned in the parking lot at the Pier. Gracie was safe in the back."

"Darn it. I'm glad you and Gracie are safe but I hate losing those guys."

"Sorry to tell you, Tom, but the burglars escaping isn't your biggest problem."

"What do you mean?"

"I mean Gracie and Spirit just found a dead body under the Pier."

* * *

By the time Lea got the dogs settled in the car, Tom had arrived. Even as she related to Tom exactly how she found the abandoned van and the dead body, the parking lot began filling with police cars and other vehicles. Before they finished their conversation, a team of crime scene personnel had begun to search the scene and collect evidence. Another officer cordoned off the area with yellow cones.

"You better hang around long enough to let them get your fingerprints, Lea. They'll be taking all the prints they can get off the van. Yours will show up because you opened the back doors to let Gracie out. Then you can go home. I'm sure Paul's worried sick. Stop by the station tomorrow to sign a statement detailing what you told me."

Lea ran her fingers through her long hair tucking it behind her ears. "What a night. The first dead body I've ever found; I hope it will be the last. At least you'll have a witness if you catch those burglars, or should I call them murderers?"

"That's the first thing I need to figure out. Whether or not these crimes were committed by the same perpetrator. Was the victim meeting the burglars and got into a confrontation that ended in them killing him? Or was he already dead when they arrived?"

"Too bad your witness can't tell us what the burglars did."

Tom scratched his head. "What witness are you talking about, Lea?"

"The four-legged one in the back of the van. At least she'll let you know if she ever sees . . . or smells . . . those guys again."

Tom smiled, looking over to where Gracie sat in the car with her head hanging out the window. "Unfortunately, her identification wouldn't hold up in a court of law, but it will sure let me know if I've found the right guys."

The Detective turned to the man approaching him. "We've identified your vic, Tom," the coroner reported. "Driver's license in his wallet says he's Neal Henderson. Age twenty-eight. Local address."

Lea overheard the coroner's remarks. "Oh, no; I know him. He worked for one of my clients."

"What can you tell us about him?"

"Not a lot. He works for Don Carson, the big real estate developer. Don's son Adam and Neal went to high school together. Football heroes at Viaje High, surfers, heartthrobs from what Don complained about. Girls used to distract both of them but his son was more studious. Neal was the Casanova."

"Do they both work for Carson?"

"No; Adam went back East to one of the Ivy League schools. He hooked up with a girlfriend and found a job there when he finished graduate school. Don thinks his son will come back here once he's married his girlfriend and they're ready to start a family.

Neal stayed out here and went to the state university. He went to see Don about a job as soon as he got his business degree. Since he was like a second son to Don, he was given a management position right away. Didn't have to work his way up the corporate ladder."

"Was there any resentment about the favoritism Don showed?"

"Not that I've heard of, but I'd be surprised if there wasn't. Don has always been one of the most influential business people in the County and his son is well liked and respected. From all accounts, Neal was considered to be a 'pretender to the throne' so to speak."

"Interesting," Tom mused, "And definitely worth looking into. There could be a motive for his murder other than the burglary."

"Besides, what possible reason would Henderson have for meeting with a gang of burglars?"

"What possible reason, indeed," Tom pondered. "Right now, I've got to get back to my crime scene investigators. See you at the station tomorrow."

Lea didn't need further convincing to get her fingerprinting done and leave the scene as quickly as possible.

Chapter Four

Driving to Valle Verde the next morning, Tom punched in Ken Crosby's address on his handheld GPS unit. He was familiar with the small town where Ken lived, but didn't recognize the name of the street Ken recited when Tom called to ask if he could stop by. Tom didn't want to call attention to the person unnecessarily by requesting that he come to the station for an interview. At the same time, Tom hoped the man might be a little more forthcoming if he was interviewed in the comfort of his own home.

Fifteen miles north of Buena Viaje, Valle Verde got its name from its location in a small valley surrounded by hills. The beauty of the terrain made it a magnet for artists, musicians, and health enthusiasts. With a population of only twelve thousand people, it boasted art galleries, boutique hotels, and a variety of artisan shops. One of the most popular weekly events was the Farmers Market held every Sunday featuring organic fruits and vegetables, local jams and honey, and homemade bakery items.

Tom rolled the car windows down and his shirt sleeves up as he drove. Being inland from the ocean made Valle Verde much hotter than coastal towns, especially during the summer when temperatures could soar over one hundred degrees. During the dry season May to November, the meaning of Valle Verde, Green Valley, was incongruous as the hills turned from verdant green to golden brown. It was still a month or two until the sizzling summer heat would arrive, but Tom knew the area was already on fire alert due to the ongoing drought the County had suffered.

Parking in the shade of a quartet of cottonwoods, the Detective took a moment to observe. Ken's house was small but the exterior was well kept: recently mowed yard, freshly painted shutters, large pots of colorful flowers on the front porch, and bird feeders hanging from the shade trees. The front yard was hemmed by a wood fence. A pop-up camper parked in the driveway appeared to be well cared for.

The man answering Tom's knock was casually dressed in jeans, plaid short-sleeved shirt, and boots. His thin but muscular physique was offset by a leathery face, probably a by-product of a profession spent mostly outdoors. Still, he appeared ten years younger than what Tom knew to be his age of seventy-one.

Opening the screen door, Ken shook hands and gestured toward the kitchen. "Come on in. I've been expecting you. Got a fresh pot of coffee brewing."

Tom inhaled the aroma of coffee beans and the rich fragrance of a jacaranda tree flowering in the back yard.

Ken poured the hot liquid into ceramic mugs and pushed one across the kitchen counter. "What kind of information have you come for?"

Appreciating Ken as a man of few words, Tom got right to the point. "I was hoping you might be able to provide some insight into Neal Henderson, the young man found murdered at the Pier. I understand you both worked for Don Carson."

Pride was obvious in Ken's voice: "I worked for Don Carson more than twenty years. I started as a worker on a construction crew and worked my way all the way to Construction Manager. I was Don's Construction Manager on more than forty projects in the County over the years, both residential and commercial."

"I understand Neal was managing Don's latest projects."

"That's right. He is . . . or maybe I should say he was." Ken motioned for Tom to follow him to the front porch.

"Don and I had always worked on projects together. Don handled the planning and financial side of it. He hired architects, arranged for financing from lenders, and went to the Planning Department to get all the Permits we needed. I was in charge of the construction side of the business. Then, Neal Henderson

28

came back to town after graduating from the state university and everything changed."

"Changed how?"

Ken tilted his chair back. "He convinced Don to restructure the company so there were two positions in the Construction Department: a Project Manager and a Construction Manager. The Project Manager oversees the administrative needs of the project, including budgeting and funding, but has an on-site Construction Manager involved in the day-to-day personnel and site supervision. Neal injected himself as the Project Manager and made me the Construction Manager."

"So you continued to oversee the day-to-day construction activities but reported to Neal?"

"You got it. He basically took over a lot of what Don used to do himself by convincing Don he should start taking it easier. Encouraged the boss to take his wife on those cruises he'd been promising her for the last several years but never found time for. He found a willing accomplice in Mary. Once she thought Don might finally have free time, she conspired with her friend at the travel agency to put enough pressure on Don he would have felt like a heel to refuse her any longer."

"But the new arrangement didn't sit well with you?"

Ken cradled his mug. "I couldn't complain. I still had my position as Construction Manager alright. But I felt Don was turning over vital parts of the business to Neal, things he should have been keeping a closer eye on. Things weren't the same."

"Was Neal hard to work for?"

"You could say that." Crossing his arms in front of his chest, he looked Tom directly in the eyes. "Don't misunderstand me. I'm not trying to speak ill of the dead. I'm only relating the facts as I saw them. To answer your question, yes, Neal was a hard man for everyone to work for."

"Hard to work for as far as being demanding or in other ways?"

29

"Having a boss who's hard to work for isn't a lot of fun, but I'm sure tough enough to do it to get the job done. But working for a boss who's dishonest and unethical, that's where I draw the line."

Tom's head jerked. He'd heard from other people about Neal being arrogant and pushy, but this was an entirely new slant. "Can you clarify?"

"Just what I said. I never had any proof to take to Don, but I'd spent too many years knowing when projects begin to run off the tracks. Like what was happening to Neal's projects. They were behind schedule and over budget. The worst thing, I suspected he was substituting cheaper materials than what the plans called for to make up for cost overruns. That kind of foolhardy move can get you in a lot of trouble when the Building Inspectors come around."

"Did you ever confront Neal with those allegations?"

"Sure I did. I mean, I didn't like the arrogant son of a gun, but I wanted him to succeed for Don's sake. Don thought of Neal as a second son, and any man wants to be proud of a son. Besides, I didn't want him to undermine Don's reputation."

"How did Neal react?"

"Not good by any definition. He ranted and raved about my questioning his abilities because I was jealous. Told me I was over the hill, out of touch with new trends in construction management. He finished by laughing, saying I couldn't prove any of it, and if I was smart, I wouldn't go around raising doubts, especially in Don's mind, about what kind of job he was doing."

Tom raised an eyebrow. "You mean he threatened you?"

"Not in so many words, but he made it clear he wasn't going to let me stand in the way of his getting to the top."

"You think he had plans to take over Don's business someday?"

"I think he saw it as a strong possibility, especially if Don's son stayed on the East Coast."

30

Tom peppered Don with more questions. "What happened between you and Neal after the confrontation? Why did you end up leaving? Were you fired or did you leave of your own volition?"

"Oh, Neal could never have taken things to that extreme. For one thing, Don would never have heard of me being fired." Ken cupped his hands behind his head. "Instead, Neal did whatever he could to make my job unpleasant. It got to the point where it wasn't fun anymore. So I told Don I was ready to retire."

"Was it true?"

"Not hardly. Don was ready to semi-retire and start traveling with Mary, but I would have worked another five years at least. I lost my wife nine years ago of cancer. My job was what I got up for in the morning." Don swallowed hard, turning his head to the side. "Like I say, once it became work and not something I loved doing, it was time to leave."

"Were you bitter about how Neal forced you out?"

"Nope. First of all, he didn't force me out. It was totally a decision I made for my own peace of mind. Secondly, Don gave me a generous retirement bonus in appreciation of all the years we'd worked together. Something totally unexpected but enough to let me devote all my time to a lifetime passion."

"Which is?" Tom asked with interest.

Ken smiled for the first time, and his eyes twinkled. "I've been flying for recreation for years but I'm doing something now I've wanted to do my whole life. I'm building my own plane from scratch. A sweet little biplane I'm building in my garage. Can't wait for the day when I take it up for the first time. May be a little scary," he chuckled, "in case I've made any mistakes. But it will be a once-in-a-lifetime thrill."

Tom laughed. "You're a braver man than me. But you've got a lot more construction knowledge than I have, too. I'm sure it will be a beauty."

* * *

31

Tom took his time getting back to the station, enjoying the view of the ocean as he drove away from the valley. He'd like to eliminate Ken Crosby as a suspect.

Ken seems like a nice guy and it appears the man has found his own sense of peace with the way things worked out at Carson's company. Or is the sense of peace I detect a result of Ken having already wreaked his revenge on the man who brought his career to an unhappy ending?

Tom knew better than to dismiss any possible suspect without reviewing means, motive, and opportunity.

Ken could have easily driven to the Pier and had a confrontation with the victim on the deserted beach without being noticed. It's easy to see Ken is an avid physical fitness practitioner. He would have had no problem overpowering Neal if circumstances so dictated.

Which brought Tom to the next question: *Could Ken have known Neal would be at the Pier that time of night? Was it merely a chance encounter between the two men, setting off a deep seated hatred and anger in Ken which led to the fatal outcome?*

Tom explored another possible motive: *Had Ken been privy to information Neal was involved in the burglaries? On the fatal night in question, was Ken looking for proof to discredit Neal for good in the eyes of Don Carson? Had things gone terribly wrong in his quest for proof?*

The Detective knew it was too early to remove Ken Crosby from his list of suspects.

* * *

The next day, Maddy waited impatiently as Lea gave the waiter at their favorite outdoor restaurant her lunch order for a Crab Louie salad and iced tea. Having heard about her sister's exciting car chase and discovery of a dead body, Maddy was now anxious to hear what news Lea had about Tom Elliot's suspect

32

list. Her perfectly shaped eyebrows rose when she heard one of the names.

"Beth Owens? Her mother, Helen, is one of my customers. When Helen remodeled, she and I spent a couple of days together picking out living and dining room furniture. I took her to the Furniture Design Center where we found several antique pieces which fit perfectly into her decor."

"Did you ever meet Beth?"

"Beth came to Helen's house one afternoon when we were trying rug samples on the floors. She's as lovely in person as the pictures five years ago when she won the title of Miss Buena Viaje."

Maddy paused momentarily while the waiter delivered their drink order. "It was around the time Beth was engaged to be married to Neal Henderson. She was gushing on to her mother and me about furnishing the new house she and Neal would be building soon after the wedding. A marriage, you'll recall, which never took place."

"The fact Neal called off the wedding days before the big event was scheduled to take place is why Beth is on Tom's list of suspects."

Maddy voiced her doubts. "Are the police implying revenge as a motive?"

"Obviously. Any woman would be mortified to be treated that way."

"The young woman I met at Helen's home didn't seem capable of anything but joy and happiness."

Maddy paused, remembering how she had changed after her own marriage ended in divorce. A shadow of pain flitted across her face as she continued. "But I know bitter disappointment can change a person completely."

Lea tried to offer reassurance. "Hopefully for her sake, it's more a matter of eliminating her from the list rather than the police seriously suspecting her capable of such a terrible act."

Maddy's face lit up. "We might be able to get information from Beth that could help remove her from the suspect list".

"How do you propose we do that?"

"By giving her an opportunity to open up about her feelings. She'll talk to us more easily than to Tom using his brusque interrogation style in the environment of the police station."

"Maybe so. But where or when will we have a chance to talk with her?"

"Tomorrow morning at the office where I have an appointment to have my teeth cleaned. Beth is the receptionist for my dentist. She may not go to work today so soon after learning of Neal's death but I'm sure by tomorrow she'll be back at work."

Maddy flashed a dazzling smile. "You can come with me and try to talk with her while the hygienist works on these pearly whites. I'm sure if you offer her a sympathetic shoulder, she'll be more than happy to cry on it."

Lea hesitated momentarily. "Neither Paul nor Tom would approve."

"If nothing comes of it, they never need to know," her sister reasoned.

"I'll admit, it does seem like your having an appointment tomorrow is fate providing an opportunity we would be lax to ignore."

"My sentiments exactly." The sisters tapped their wine glasses.

* * *

Tom flashed his badge as he pulled up to the security gate at the condominium complex where Neal had lived. "Any unusual activity?" he asked the guard.

"No, sir. It's been quiet ever since the police finished with Mr. Henderson's unit. There have only been a couple of non-

34

residents to the complex the last two days. A Federal Express delivery and a guy with a pest control company."

"Good luck if he's spraying for ants in the common areas. No one can get rid of them this year because of the drought."

"Told me he was responding to a call from one of the residents complaining about bees."

Tom paused. "Which unit did he go to?"

"Let me check the log." Moments later, a red-faced guard returned. "The guy signed in, but his handwriting is illegible. I remember him though. He was wearing a uniform with an emblem of a bug on the front, and he had a backpack sprayer. Looked like a pest company alright."

Tom's eyes squinted and his jaw jutted out, the usual sign of the Detective's displeasure. "I'm going to unit 302 if any officers come looking for me."

Located adjacent to the boardwalk, the complex afforded most of the units an ocean view. The building was Spanish Colonial architecture complete with orange tile roofs and whitewashed walls. The grounds were well maintained with plush green grass, palm trees, and colorful rose bushes on either side of a stone walkway leading to the front entrance.

But Tom was in no mood to be impressed by the beauty of the building. By the time he parked his car and rode the elevator to the third floor, he was quite certain of what he would find.

It should have been easy to spot unit 302 with crime scene tape crisscrossed across the door, except the crime scene tape had been torn off and the lock had been jimmied. Walking through the rooms, it was obvious to Tom someone had been desperately searching for something. Desk drawers in the study were pulled out and turned upside down. Papers were strewn over the floor. Books torn off the shelves. In the kitchen, cereal boxes, cans, and jars had been pulled out of the cupboards. Clothes had been ripped out of drawers in the bedroom and pulled off hangers in the closet.

35

Tom wasted no time calling his squad with news of his discovery. He gave instructions for a technician to be sent to dust for fingerprints.

"It could be someone trying to destroy evidence of a connection to the murder victim. Which means it could be the burglars, or it could be the murderer, depending on whether the burglars and the murderer are one and the same."

"Has the safe been broken into?" asked the detective on the other end of the call.

Neal glanced at the intact floor safe. "From the scratches around the latch, it looks like someone tried. If it was the burglars, they could have been looking for Henderson's take from the burglaries. They'll need plenty of money if they have to stay on the run. We'll find out when the tech runs the prints if they match those we got from the van."

"Or it could have been Neal Henderson's murderer?"

"Exactly. That makes running prints even more compelling."

Tom hung up and finished his inspection on the balcony. Complete with hot tub. *Boy, this guy had it all.*

He looked at the beach and listened to the pounding of the breaking surf. *Must be nice to sit in your spa enjoying a beer and a view of the ocean at the end of the day. It would almost be enough to wish you had a job where you could come home at night.*

Shaking his head, Tom took a last glance at the brilliant orange and red of the setting sun reflected in the ocean. *And this jerk lost everything, including his life, trying to get more.*

Returning to the living room to wait for the fingerprint tech, his eyes came to rest on a picture frame on the floor. The glass was broken. Tom picked up a jaggedly torn picture lying next to it. What was left of the picture showed the victim wearing a tuxedo standing in front of a red Mercedes-Benz. He was attending some fancy bash from the look of the other people in the picture, all

36

dressed to the hilt including women laden with expensive jewelry. Tom didn't recognize any of the people shown walking into a building with their backs to the camera. The setting looked familiar but he couldn't immediately place it.

Who's in the part of the picture torn away? Did someone worry enough about being seen with Neal to go to this much trouble? Or was destroying the picture an act of angry jealousy?

As he started to replace the frame on the table, he noticed the hinge on the back. His pulse skipped a beat as he opened it. Behind the mat board was a scrap of paper with numbers written on it and another picture. *Are these numbers the combination to a safe or a locker?* He quickly tried the numbers on the floor safe with no luck.

The picture was of an attractive woman smiling at the victim. Tom understood why Neal may have been reluctant to display a picture of himself embracing this woman so soon after his broken nuptials. The woman in the picture was decidedly not Beth Owens.

Chapter Five

"First burglary, then murder," Paul muttered, arriving for a meeting with the client whose project had been the springboard to Lea's discovery of a dead body. Parking in an unpaved lot, he opened the door of a mobile trailer that served as the construction office.

One of two men bent over a drawing board looked up as Paul entered. "Come in, Paul. Give me a moment."

Paul looked out the window at the flurry of activity on the nearly completed project. It was one of the things he loved about the development business. All the pieces coming together to turn an architect's renderings into reality.

He watched as his client rolled up a set of plans and dropped it into a storage tube, dismissing the man next to him with a slap on the back: "Good work, Bill. On schedule and under budget. I can't ask for more."

Paul's client waved him through to one of the offices in the trailer. "There's table and chairs in here where we can talk."

Jim Mitchell was of the same athletic build as Paul but the older man looked taller and leaner in the confined space of the construction trailer. Paul usually saw his client at his more lavish showroom offices downtown.

"Thanks for agreeing to meet me here on the site."

"No problem, Jim. I know how busy you are." Paul lowered his own six-foot frame into one of the metal chairs. "How are you holding up? The burglary at Two Palms Sunday night was bad enough. Have you been able to get back on track since the robbery at the residential site yesterday?"

"Yeah, I've got a great foreman and two good crews." Jim pushed his chair back from the table to give himself more leg room. "They're used to working through unexpected on-site problems. Biggest distraction at the residential project has been the news van hovering most of the day."

"I'm afraid you have my wife to thank for bringing so much attention since the news media linked the burglary and the murder."

"I'm just sorry she went through the experience of finding a dead body."

"It was none of your doing. Full responsibility for her being in a position to find a dead body rests with our overly zealous border collie."

Paul reached for the bottled water Jim offered. "But why are the media people still pursuing the case? I thought the police had pretty much determined the burglary on your site and the body found at the Pier aren't linked."

"That's what Detective Elliot told me during our interview about the burglary. But once the television station reported the crimes as being linked, it was hard to get them to change their angle," Jim complained. "I even had people asking me if the body was found on our construction site. We sure don't need that kind of bad publicity for future sales purposes."

"I hear you, Jim, but I'm sure you didn't call me today about a public relations issue."

"No." He walked over to close the office door.

"Part of your consulting service for my real estate business has been to help me with personnel issues like screening job candidates. In this case, I'm hoping you can provide a needed third party perspective on another kind of personnel issue."

"Glad to help any way I can."

"I have an employee I'd like you to speak with. I don't think this young man will open up to me as his boss, but I'm hoping he might be more forthcoming with a neutral third party."

"What's the problem?"

"One of our young construction workers got in a bit of trouble last week. Right now, it sort of boils down to helping me clear any doubts I, or anyone on the crew, has about his character."

"Why is his character in question?"

"I need to make sure he didn't have anything to do with the burglaries which have been going on."

Paul's jaw dropped. "You better give me all the details. What kind of trouble did this young man get into?"

"Our site manager noticed small tools disappearing from one of our projects. Gloves, hammers, screwdrivers, safety glasses, basically, small stuff it's hard to keep track of. He didn't bring it to my attention until a couple of power drills were reported missing."

"How do you keep track of your equipment?"

"I'll admit, we're a little outdated in that department. Our equipment is always moving from our main warehouse to multiple job sites as needed. Quite frankly, it gets lost or stolen all too often.

Basically, we use sign out sheets at the main warehouse to keep track of which construction worker has what piece of equipment, at which location, and for how long. A paper trail isn't available in the field until the clerical staff has the time to transfer the information into a spreadsheet the site managers can then access on their computer."

"If your site manager didn't have access to the inventory list at the job site, how did he find out about the power drills?"

"From crew members complaining about equipment not being available. When he went to the warehouse and cross checked inventory checked out against inventory checked in, he discovered the smaller items, plus the drills, missing."

"Does your site manager have any ideas about who might have taken the missing items?"

"He does, in fact. He suspects the young man in question, Juan Martinez."

"Can't you confront Juan with your suspicions?"

"Typically, I would, but that's why I've asked for your intercession. John, my site manager, is good at what he does but he sometimes demonstrates a bit of a bias against young Hispanics."

"Awkward, considering the large proportion of Hispanics working on your projects."

"Yes, it can be. From what I know of Juan's background, he never finished high school, another strike in John's estimation. I want to make sure there's adequate reason to suspect Juan before I cause him undue embarrassment by accusing him."

"I understand your position and I think you're right. It could be unfair to the young man. It could also expose you to a claim of wrongful termination if the situation gets out of hand. Hopefully, it won't come to that if I can get Juan to be open enough to decide if there's any merit in John's suspicion."

"I appreciate it, Paul. Take whatever time you need with Juan and bill me." Jim lowered his voice as he opened the door. "I sincerely hope you'll find no reason to pursue this further. I've seen Juan on the job and know him to be a hard-working, personable young man."

"I hope the results of my interview are favorable to Juan as well, but I'll be giving you an honest evaluation."

"I'd expect no less." Jim put on his sunglasses. "Juan's working on this site today. I'll have his supervisor radio him to come to the trailer. Want to grab lunch when you're finished?"

"Thanks, but Lea has reservations at The Apex. I'm going to meet her at twelve."

"Can't imagine you turning me down for that beautiful wife of yours. Send me your report."

* * *

To prevent undue suspicion being cast on Juan, Jim and Paul had agreed the interview would be camouflaged as screening to select a construction crew for an upcoming new project. The foreman hadn't been informed of the real purpose of the interview and expressed skepticism about Juan being considered for the new crew. Jim had dismissed John's concerns.

The worker who entered the construction trailer was tall and lanky. He was a handsome young man with black hair, a high forehead, and bushy eyebrows framing dark luminous eyes. He walked toward Paul with his hand outstretched, flashing a broad smile exposing teeth that could have been in a toothpaste commercial.

"Juan Martinez, sir. I'm glad to meet you."

"Likewise, Juan." Paul gestured to the other chair. "Please, call me Paul. Would you like something cold to drink?"

"Thank you. It's heating up pretty good out there." He held the soda can against his forehead for a moment.

"Construction work can be grueling," Paul suggested, hoping to get a read on whether Juan liked his job.

"Yeah, but it pays well. And it's outdoors. I could never work in an office all day." Juan took a long gulp of the frosty beverage, flashing another broad smile.

"What did you study in school?"

"I didn't make it to college. I had to drop out of high school before I got my diploma." Juan stared at the floor.

"Trouble at school?" Paul asked casually. He watched the young man's face and hands closely.

Juan fidgeted slightly in his chair, taking a moment before responding as if making up his mind about how to answer. He lifted his head to make eye contact with Paul. His response was blunt; his countenance determined and confident. "I had plans to go to junior college here in town. I was saving money to go to State University and get a degree in business."

"What stopped you from getting your diploma?"

"My Mom has bad back problems. She used to work in a laundry, standing all day. After that, she had a job working for a house cleaning service in town. She started taking pills for the pain and to help her sleep. The last couple months of my senior year, the drugs she was taking got out of hand. A dealer was supplying her with narcotics and she got addicted. She ended up at the hospital on an overdose. I had to drop out of school to take care of my little brothers and sisters. When she came home from the hospital, she was sick from the withdrawal for weeks and couldn't start working again. I was the only one old enough to earn money."

"That's tough. Where was your father while all this was going on?"

Juan snickered, shifting his long legs under the table. "Haven't seen the dude since I was four years old. He took off after my younger brother was born. My other brother and two sisters have different fathers. Not one stuck around. My Mom's done it all on her own," he said, adding softly, "with the help of welfare, and me."

"Quite a load for a young man to carry, helping your mom with the finances." Paul needed to figure out if the need to support his mother and provide for his siblings was pushing him to steal materials he could resell.

"It's taught me one thing for sure," he said angrily. "When I have a family someday, I'll never desert them. It's a coward's way of living. I'll teach my kids to accept the responsibility that comes with having children. I see too many of my friends having babies way too early before they have a way to support them."

"It sounds like you used everything you learned from a difficult situation to turn yourself into an outstanding young man."

"I hope so. It's why I need to keep working construction right now. It pays me enough so I can help my mom and still save money to get my high school diploma and enroll at the junior college. I'm planning to take night classes and still work during the day."

"Ambitious program, young man. One I believe you're capable of accomplishing."

Paul stood to bring the conversation to a close. Putting his arm over Juan's shoulder as they walked to the door, he asked casually: "By the way, do you have any ideas on who has been pulling off the burglaries in the last couple of weeks?"

Juan turned to face Paul. Paul's heart was in his throat, afraid he might hear a response from Juan that could implicate him.

"Hey, man, those burglaries are bad business. Personally, I think it has to be an inside job." He pinched his lower lip between his thumb and forefinger, deep in thought. "I mean, it seems like these guys know which sites are the easiest to hit. They hit at exactly the right time when the security guard is away from the front gate doing his rounds. It's like they know the schedule."

"Do guards follow a definite routine?"

"Oh, yeah. In fact, there's a machine on the site where the guards log their inspections. It's the boss' way to make sure the guard makes his rounds when he's supposed to and covers the whole property." Juan grinned. "Without the logging machine, the guy could just stand out in back somewhere having a smoke."

An alarm sounded in the back of Paul's mind. "You seem to know quite a bit about the routine."

"I've worked as a security guard. I know exactly how it works. I've also worked at a car wash, flipping burgers at a drive-through, and parking cars at the country club." Juan patted his chest. "I'm a man of all trades, you might say."

"How do you like working for Jim Mitchell's company?"

"I respect Mr. Mitchell a lot. His foreman is strict but fair; he knows how to treat us guys in the field right so we want to do a good job for him."

Paul sensed Juan's sincerity and liked the young man more and more as the conversation progressed. But his next statement made Paul catch his breath. "Believe me, it's a lot better than working for Neal Henderson."

"When did you work for Neal, Juan?"

"Right before I came over here. I was only on Mr. Henderson's job for a month or so when he suddenly let me go for no reason. Man, I was upset. I needed the money, and I was doing a good job."

"What reason did he give for terminating you?"

"He talked about tools gone missing on the site. He never accused me of stealing, but he said stuff started being reported right after I was hired and it was making me look bad." His eyebrows squeezed together and his jaw jutted out. "It was all a big misunderstanding. I swear I'd never do anything like that no matter how bad I needed money. I'm not dumb enough to do something stupid so I end up in jail when I've got my family to take care of. It was all unfair."

"Did you have any trouble finding another job after you were let go?"

"That was the strange part. Mr. Henderson told me he would show on my personnel records I was terminated because the job was winding down so I'd be able to find other work. In fact, he was the one who told me they needed construction workers here on Mr. Mitchell's project."

Paul relaxed. Juan's candor and honesty were hardly synonymous with someone trying to cover up criminal activities. But before he concluded the interview, he took the opportunity to dispel one last lingering doubt.

His next question was not aimed at anything Jim Mitchell had asked him to pursue but something he needed to know for his own peace of mind. "I guess working a full-time job and helping your Mom take care of your siblings, you don't have much time to yourself," Paul suggested.

"Yeah, I keep pretty busy. But don't worry; I find time for the important stuff like watching the Lakers game against the

Spurs with my buddies Monday night. I still can't believe they won the game. One of their best comebacks ever."

"Unfortunately, I missed a lot of the game. At least I saw the final minutes when the Lakers made a run of a dozen points." Paul didn't bother to tell Juan the reason he was unable to watch much of the game was because his wife was busy discovering a dead body at the Pier. He was relieved to have assured himself that even though Juan Martinez may have had a possible motive in being unfairly terminated by the victim, he had a solid alibi for the time of the murder.

"I wish you the best, Juan. You're a godsend to your mother and you're on the right path with your life. Keep working hard. I'm sure you'll get a diploma and whatever else you set your sights on." Paul shook Juan's hand, clapping him on the shoulder.

"Thank you. It means a lot to have people believe in me."

As Juan headed back to work, Paul hoped what he had learned would be enough to convince Tom that Juan Martinez was not the one who killed Neal Henderson.

Chapter Six

Lea entered the Carson Building and walked over to the snack stand. The twenty-one story building was the tallest structure in town. The front entrance boasted a circular drive with a water fountain. Across the parking lot was a small retail center hosting a Starbucks, sandwich shop, copy store, and FedEx.

The first floor of the office building included a bank, an insurance company, and an employment agency. Don Carson housed the divisions of his development company on floors eighteen through twenty. The top floor included a penthouse reserved for Don and his assistants, and The Apex, the County's premier members club known for its outstanding cuisine, sky lounge, and banquet facilities. With a breathtaking view of the ocean, The Apex was the meeting place of choice for business, political, and social leaders.

"Hey, Bobby. How's it going?" She pulled a bottle of cold water from the refrigerator and picked up a package of breath mints from the counter.

"I'm wonderful, Miss Lea." The owner of the kiosk was on a first name basis with everyone who walked into the building except the owner, whom he always called Mr. Carson out of respect. "Another sunny day in paradise. My grandkids coming for a visit. Everything is good."

"How long will they stay?"

"Two weeks. Plenty of time for me to talk my daughter and son-in-law into moving here. "

Lea laughed. "Or for them to talk you into moving back to the Philippines. We'd hate to lose you."

His broad smile exposed broken teeth. "Don't worry. My wife would never hear of it. Besides, how could Mr. Carson keep this big building running smoothly without me?"

"Things probably aren't running too smoothly today with the news about Neal Henderson."

"It's terrible. All the tenants are buzzing. The police and reporters were here earlier. Mr. Carson was out of town, but I saw his helicopter landing on the helipad when I came in at seven o'clock. "

"Neal was his right-hand man. He'll have a lot to take on."

"Maybe Adam will come home now. It's too bad such a terrible thing should be the reason, but everyone would be happy to see that happen."

"I'm sure Adam will do what he thinks is best for all concerned. From what I hear, he has a girlfriend on the East Coast to consider."

"Rumor is she's from an old school, old money family. She may not be ready to settle down in a small laid back West Coast town." The old man's eyes twinkled. "If she's worried about that, she doesn't know how Mr. Carson lives."

"I'm sure you could give her the lowdown, Bobby," Lea laughed. "I've got to run."

"Which of your clients are you here to see?"

"Going to The Apex. Angelo needs brochures for the next Food Fest."

"I've heard about his cooking competitions. The people who go the last day sample the winner's dishes. Dishes fit for a king."

"Maybe I can get you a ticket."

"Oh, thank you, Miss Lea, but don't bother. It would be too rich for my stomach. I'm used to my wife's simple Filipino fare. She doesn't let me eat fancy stuff. Says it will clog my arteries."

"She's a smart woman, Bobby. You listen to her."

"Don't worry. I have no choice." He turned to help his next customer.

* * *

48

It was only eleven o'clock, but the restaurant was bustling. "Busy day, Angelo?" Lea asked the handsome, stylishly dressed owner of The Apex when he appeared from the kitchen.

"Both lunch seatings are booked."

"I'm glad I made reservations yesterday. I talked my husband into treating me to lunch after you and I finish. I may have forgotten to call today with all the excitement of the murder."

"We've had a number of last minute reservations. I think people are coming to gossip."

"Neal must have been a regular at your restaurant. Did you know him well?"

"As well as I wanted to. The thing that happened was terrible, but I don't think anyone who knew him is shedding tears. He wasn't a pleasant young man. His arrogance was offensive and he could be childishly petty."

"Surely he would never have been rude to you, knowing what a close friend of Don Carson you are."

"That didn't stop him one night a few weeks ago. It was a Tuesday, typically a slow night for us. Neal and a lady friend were here for dinner. Everyone knows we close at ten o'clock during the week. It was obvious he and the woman were wrapped up in each other at closing time. Neal wanted me to accommodate them. Acting like a big shot by having the restaurant stay open. No way was I going to cater to him. The only person I stay open for after hours is Don Carson.

The waiter had closed out their dinner ticket. I told Neal he needed to leave. When he didn't, I turned out the lights. The woman laughed and told Neal it was time to go. She was quite nice about the whole thing but Neal was livid.

The next day half way through the lunch hour, the building had a fire drill. It was not a big deal for the other tenants. Most of them were taking their lunch break. For me, it was a disaster. Many of my customers had to leave hot meals. By the time they returned, their food was cold. I offered to reheat plates for people

49

with hot entrees, but most of them didn't have time. They left with their food half eaten. I'm sure he did it to spite me for what happened the night before."

Lea cocked her head. "Don't worry, Lea. Italians are known for our fiery tempers, but he didn't get under my skin enough for me to kill him. I can't speak for some of the others he offended."

"What about the woman he was with that night? Do you know if that was a serious relationship?"

"Oh, heavens, no. At least, I wouldn't think so. She's older and married."

"I assumed it was a date from the way you described their intimacy."

"Their exchange was more intense than intimate. But if what you assumed is correct, that would, indeed, make for juicy gossip."

"Why, Angelo?"

"Neal was with City Councilwoman, Margaret Patton."

* * *

Seated at a table next to the picture window, Lea waited impatiently for Paul.

Scheduling a meeting with Angelo while lunch was being prepared had not been smart. The chef dedicated each day of the week to a different kind of cuisine. Today, barbecue was featured. Her taste buds were salivating from the tantalizing smells of brisket cooking: chili powder, garlic, onion, peppers, and bay leaf.

Her meeting with Angelo had gone well. She was sketching ideas for the brochure on her notepad when a hand moving across her back sent chills up her neck.

"Could this gorgeous red-head be my lunch date?"

"Don't tell your wife. I hear she's slaving away making a living. She'd envy you frittering your time away over martinis in this magnificent setting."

50

"Does that mean you've already ordered?"

"It was a no-brainer. After smelling the lunch special for the last hour, I had no choice but to order it."

By the time the entrée arrived, they had finished their drinks and discussed morning activities.

Paul lifted a large forkful of mashed potatoes to his mouth. "Gordon Parks was in the elevator when I came up. Asked if I was ready to join his firm."

"And . . . ?"

"I gave him the same no I give him each time he asks."

She let out the breath she was holding. "You have to give him credit. He's persistent."

"He's persisting in a losing cause. I've told him I have no interest in becoming a broker."

"Doesn't he do leasing for several of your clients?"

"Yep, and that's the way I like it. He contracts with my clients to take care of their major leasing needs. I take care of their development and management needs. I do renewals for existing tenants, but that's all I want of leasing. The brokerage business is too competitive for me. Too cut-throat."

"Gordon isn't that way, is he?"

"Not particularly. But a couple of the brokers working for him have no qualms about cutting other brokers out so they don't have to share commissions. One, in particular, has earned the nickname Trickster for the number of deals he's cheated other brokers on."

"Why doesn't Gordon stop it?"

"He takes a hands-off attitude. Expects brokers to negotiate commissions on their own."

"But isn't the payment of commissions one of the terms in the listing agreement?"

"Much of the language in a contract is subject to interpretation. The Trickster has ways of spinning the interpretation so he ends up with the biggest slice of the pie."

"I can easily see why you couldn't work in that kind of environment. You always look for the win-win in every deal."

"I've never been willing to push the boundaries on honest business practices. I never got over the developer I worked for when we lived in San Diego. Remember him?"

"How could I forget? The one who wanted you to represent to a lender that a project would yield a higher return than was possible."

"That's the one. Tried to convince me a slight fudging of the numbers wouldn't hurt anyone. Promised me a bonus when the loan got approved."

"You asked how you could sleep at night if you started cheating to line your own pockets. He insisted bankers were just as bad."

"Unfortunately, he was right. But other people's greed and corruption isn't an excuse. It's a personal choice. A decision to go down that road is usually made without consideration for how innocent people may be affected. The greed of big business and the attitude that corruption is acceptable because everyone's doing it led to the economic collapse."

"From what I'm hearing, greed and ego were qualities that may have led to Neal Henderson's downfall."

Lea started to recap her conversation with Angelo but decided not to risk ruining a perfect lunch by alerting Paul to her interest in the murder victim.

* * *

Tom was at the Carson Building to talk with Don's Property Manager, Brad Johnson. The management office on the eighteenth floor was modestly but tastefully furnished. Presenting his credentials at the front desk, Tom was ushered into an office containing a desk littered with files.

52

"I paged Brad," the secretary informed him. "He's with an electrician, but he's on his way. Would you like a cup of coffee?"

"Yes, thanks."

The Property Manager arrived before the coffee. The secretary returned with two cups, one which she placed in front of the harried young man. He dropped a pager, clipboard, and sunglasses on top of the papers on his desk.

"Thanks, Ann. No calls, please. I don't care what emergency someone tells you they're having."

Tom leaned across the desk with his card. "Thanks for seeing me without an appointment, Mr. Johnson."

"Please, call me Brad. No thanks needed. Appointments are for the bigwigs upstairs. Everyone barges in our office unannounced. I'm glad of the chance to take an uninterrupted break," he said, exhaling a deep breath.

"I'm investigating the death of Neal Henderson. Did you and Mr. Henderson work together?"

"No. Neal handled the construction side of Don's business. I'm strictly Property Management, taking care of the tenants and the maintenance on all the properties. I saw him at the company meetings once a week. Other than that, I made it a point to steer clear of him."

"You didn't like him?"

"I don't know many people who did. He was a jackass. Arrogant. Always throwing his weight around. Meddling in things outside his department."

"Such as?"

"Telling my security guards or maintenance crew how to do their jobs. He couldn't walk through the building without having a few choice words about windows needing to be washed or a car in the parking lot without a permit that security should tag. Other department heads would never do that. They know better. I don't tell the leasing guys how to do their jobs and I would never butt in with a general contractor."

53

"Why do you think Don Carson thought highly of him if other people, yourself included, had a bad opinion of him?"

"Henderson was a brown-noser. He made sure Mr. Carson always saw him at his best. Acted like everyone's bosom buddy when the boss was around. Tried to give the impression he was well liked by the employees. Dished out accolades in front of Carson, then turned around and chewed out the same person the next day."

"Why didn't anyone tell Carson the employees didn't like him?"

"Nobody wanted to hurt the boss. They knew Neal was a substitute son while his own son was back East. We all figured Neal would leave once Adam came back and he realized he was never going to take over Don's business."

"Did you have any run-ins with Neal?"

"I saw him in his car in the parking garage after hours one night making out with one of the secretaries who works at the insurance company."

"That was hardly company business. Why did you care?"

His voice got louder. "Because he was engaged to Beth Owens at the time. He had no right to be doing what he was doing."

"I repeat, why did you care?"

"I live next door to Beth. We grew up together. Neal was cheating on her. I didn't want to see her hurt by that moron."

"Big brother steps in to save his sister's honor?"

The anguish in Brad's face told Tom this was a case of more than brotherly love.

"You're in love with Beth." It was a statement, not a question.

Brad's shoulders drooped. He turned his head to one side. "Since the first day of high school. We were like brother and sister through elementary school. In middle school, we were more like best friends, hung out in the same group. We talked about people

54

we had crushes on and gave each other advice. Freshman year of high school, it all changed for me. I started seeing her differently. I fell really hard."

"Did she feel the same way?"

He laughed. "Not even close. I was a big brother, best friend, and confidante. Nothing more in her eyes."

"Didn't you tell her how you felt?"

"She hooked up with Neal before I had a chance. Apart from break-ups which happened every few months, they were a steady couple through high school and university. I wasn't surprised when I heard they were engaged. Everyone expected them to get married."

"Weren't you happy for her?"

"I would have been. Once I knew she'd never feel about me the way I felt about her, I only wanted her to be happy. But she was never going to be happy with that jerk. He was incapable of caring for anyone but himself."

"What happened when you confronted Neal?"

"I waited until the next day. Around noon, I saw him standing alone by the fountain at the front entrance. I didn't mince my words. Came right out and told him I saw him in the garage cheating on Beth."

"How'd he react?"

"He burst out laughing. Told me I needed to get over my pathetic big brother complex. Said she was a big girl. If she had a problem with the way he acted, she'd tell him herself."

The muscles in Brad's neck pulsed. His fists doubled. "I pushed the guy. Walked right over and shoved him as hard as I could. Trying to knock the smirk off his face."

"Did he push back?"

"Hard enough to knock me off balance. I fell backward into the fountain. I can still see the obnoxious look on his face when I stood up in the middle of the fountain, clothes dripping, hair mussed, glasses water stained. He doubled over in laughter, turned, and walked away. I wanted to kill him."

Chapter Seven

Tom rode the elevator to the penthouse suite. Pushing open a large oak door, he walked into a plush reception area. The office was fitting for a developer, showing off lots of tinted glass, recessed lighting, and wood paneling.

"Tom Elliot here to see Amanda Hughes."

"She told me you were coming, Mr. Elliot. Amanda's in with Mr. Carson at the moment, but she should be out momentarily. Would you care to wait in the conference room?" She gestured toward a large room at the front of the building.

Entering the room, Tom was met with a sweeping vista provided by floor to ceiling glass windows. Depending on which direction he looked, he had a view of the city straight ahead, the mountains to the right, and the ocean including the Pier and the Boardwalk to the left. He imagined what it would be like to work in an office with this view.

The voice behind him echoed his thoughts. "Sometimes it's hard to focus on my work with that view in front of me. I'm new to the top floor. I'm not used to all this grandeur yet."

The young woman extended her hand: "Amanda Hughes. Sorry to keep you waiting. Mr. Carson is getting ready to take another trip so I needed to get his signature on some papers before he leaves town." She gestured for Tom to sit across from her.

"No problem. Does he travel frequently?"

"When Neal was here . . ." her voice faltered and she lowered her head. "Sorry, I'm not used to Neal's being gone."

She composed herself and continued. "Mr. Carson felt comfortable leaving the operations to Neal so he's been traveling more in the last two years, taking his wife to places she's wanted to visit: Asia, Europe, and Alaska."

57

"Must be quite a treat for the two of them."

"If I can be candid, I think after the first trip, Mr. Carson would have preferred to stay home. He enjoys working more than sitting down to full-dress dinners on cruise ships and visiting art galleries in Italy. But his wife sacrificed a lot during the years Mr. Carson built his business. He feels he owes it to her.

He comes home from those trips saying 'at least my wife exposes me to culture. Whether or not it rubs off is still open for debate.' He has a wonderful sense of humor, one of the reasons people love working for him."

"How do you happen to be working for Mr. Carson now? I know you were Neal's Administrative Assistant which is why I've called on you today."

"After what happened to Neal," Tom noticed she still couldn't bring herself to refer to it as murder, "I was expecting to be looking for a position with another company. Mr. Carson was kind enough to insist I come up to this floor and work as an additional assistant for him. He knew he would be assuming areas Neal had been supervising. He felt I could be a big help to him since I had worked so closely with Neal."

"How is it working out?"

"I love working for Mr. Carson. His other assistant was very welcoming. We've become close already. I was so grateful to be able to stay with the company. I've made friends here and would have hated to leave."

"You say Mr. Carson is good to work for. From what I've heard, Neal was quite the opposite. You probably knew Neal as well as anyone in the company. Tell me, Amanda, how would you describe him?"

She took her time before answering. "Even though Mr. Carson is the owner of the company, he's kind and friendly. So approachable. Always willing to listen, offer advice, or to help. He's there for his employees in a genuine way. Neal was aloof, not the kind anyone would go to with a problem."

58

Tom sensed her reluctance. "You're not being disloyal, Amanda. Anything you tell me about Neal may help me figure out a situation he got into which ultimately resulted in his death."

Reassured, she continued: "An example might be the easiest way for you to understand how Neal saw things. One Monday morning, a group of us were in the parking lot before work admiring the new sports car the manager of the leasing department bought over the weekend. Neal broke in and slapped the guy on the back, saying something like 'Nice wheels, Bob. Bet you feel a lot better getting rid of the old beater you were driving. Just like clothes make the man, everybody judges you by the car you drive.' After he left, we all broke out laughing. None of us bases how we feel about ourselves on if we're driving the right car."

"I can understand how material possessions would be important to a man like him."

"Image is what was important to Neal. Material possessions were the means to creating the image he wanted."

"He had a reputation for being difficult and demanding to work for."

Amanda stiffened. "Who told you that?"

"It seems to be the general census of opinion."

The young woman's shoulders relaxed in resignation. "He expected a lot of the people who worked under him. He was somewhat of a perfectionist himself and wouldn't accept less than one-hundred-ten-percent effort from anyone. He got especially upset if projects were behind schedule or over budget."

"A frequent occurrence with Neal's projects?"

"It happens to everyone, but bringing projects in on time and under budget is a big part of the construction business. Neal took it personally if his projects failed to meet the goals set by Mr. Carson and the other investors. He felt it reflected on his reputation in the industry."

59

"Would you say he was willing to go to extremes to protect his reputation?"

Amanda frowned. "What exactly are you implying?"

"We're following leads suggesting Neal was involved in the construction burglaries around the County. Apparently, he needed money to cover shortfalls in the projects he was supervising."

Her response was not as adamant or as immediate as Tom anticipated.

"I'm not in any position to respond to those allegations. I can tell you Neal was under a great deal of stress in the weeks preceding his death."

"Trouble with his projects?"

"He did, in fact, have two projects going sideways. An apartment building and a mixed-use project. First, there were problems with materials not being delivered on time. Then the General Contractor walked off the job and Neal had to hire a replacement, putting him weeks behind schedule. With all the construction work going on in the County, most contractors have work lined up years in advance, especially the good ones. You don't just put an ad in the paper and find the perfect candidate."

"Why did the Contractor quit before the projects were completed?"

"He and Neal didn't get along. They argued incessantly. The last inspection on one of the projects didn't pass code compliance standards. When the Final Permit was denied, Neal really lost it. From reports we got, he went ballistic and reamed the Contractor out in front of his crew. The Contractor said he'd had enough. Walked out and took his entire crew with him."

"Did Neal try to get him back?"

"Sure he did. But as soon as the news got out, one of the other builders got hold of the Contractor and put his crew to work the next day. He gave an added enticement of a bonus if the project was completed before the due date."

"Are incentives unusual in the industry?"

"Bonuses aren't standard. They're usually given for exceptional jobs or when a contractor has put in extra effort. Neal never gave a bonus. He sometimes implied a bonus would be given but he always found a reason not to award it."

"Did Neal get Final Permits on the projects?"

"Yes, he worked it out. I'm not sure how he managed it, but he came in one morning saying everything had been taken care of and we were back on schedule. He seemed overly pleased with himself. Told us we could begin leasing and pre-selling on both projects which meant the money would start rolling in again."

Tom took out his notepad. "Do you know the exact day Neal told you the Permits were issued?"

Amanda hesitated. "Let me check my computer. I remember entering an item in my calendar to tell the Marketing Department about the completion of the projects so they could schedule an advertising campaign."

She returned with her laptop, sitting next to Tom where they could both view the screen. When she found the note to the Marketing Department, the color drained out of her face.

"What's wrong, Amanda?"

"The morning Neal told me everything would be alright again was the day he was murdered."

"Anyone besides contractors Neal fell out with?"

Amanda narrowed her eyes. "There was one unusual incident a couple of months ago. Neal fired one of our in-house construction workers."

"What do you mean in-house?"

"The way the company is structured now, Neal as Construction Manager supervises a Project Manager or contracts the work out to a General Contractor. General Contractors bid on each project and the job is awarded to the Contractor with the best bid. In Neal's mind, the best bid was usually equivalent to the cheapest bid. Before he came, we only had a Project Manager on the payroll of Carson Development Company who reported directly to Mr. Carson."

"Ken Crosby?"

Amanda seemed surprised that Tom had that information. "Yes. Ken managed projects for Mr. Carson for years. Neal consolidated the title of Project Manager into his own job description since the company was only doing a single project at a time. When business picked up and the company started doing multiple projects again, Neal started hiring a General for each individual project, leaving him in the position of supervising the Generals on all the projects."

"Sounds like a lot of work for one person."

"It is, but believe me; Neal gets enough hard work from everyone working under him to get the job done."

"And make himself look good in the eyes of his boss?"

The young woman looked at the floor, displaying a reluctance to agree with Tom's assessment of her former boss.

"So where do in-house construction workers fit in?"

"We have a crew of five or six workers who do tenant improvement work in our buildings. When a tenant negotiates a new lease, they typically ask the landlord for an allowance to expand or improve their office space. The tenant and landlord agree on an amount the landlord is willing to spend for the improvements. Most tenants lack the experience to deal with the design and construction process so they hire the landlord's Construction Department to do the actual work. The landlord has a list of trades familiar with the building and knows the ins and outs of local agencies involved in the Permit process. The employee who was fired worked on Tenant Improvement construction. He was on the payroll of Carson Development Company."

"Did Neal supervise the in-house construction workers?"

"No, he didn't. That was the odd thing. It wasn't his position to hire or fire those employees. Tenant Improvement Construction is a whole separate department. They office in a different building next to the equipment warehouse."

"So how did Neal get involved?"

"That department was experiencing minor thefts of equipment at the time. Employee theft of small amounts of materials isn't highly unusual in this business. It's like office workers taking pens, paper clips, or notepads home with them at night. Neal told the head of the Tenant Improvement Department he had received information on who might be responsible. He told the Department Supervisor he lacked definite proof so preferred to handle the matter discreetly himself. The next thing I knew he had fired one of the employees."

"Which one?"

"Juan Martinez. That was one of the most surprising things. Juan's a great kid. Everyone liked him a lot. He was one of my personal favorites. Whenever he was working in our building, he stopped in to give me a wave and a big smile. Sort of a flirt, really, but in a cute way."

"So what was given as the cause for termination?"

"It went in his employee file as termination for lack of work instead of firing. Neal actually dictated a letter of recommendation for me to prepare for Juan. It was like he wanted Juan out of this company, but he wanted to make sure he found employment somewhere else."

"Seems like a generous thing for him to do considering the circumstances."

"Yes, it was, and completely out of character for him. He avoided personnel issues like the plague. He rarely wrote a letter of recommendation and never for someone at Juan's level of employment."

"I've been informed Juan was not given a reason for his termination and did not understand why it happened."

Amanda hesitated. "That statement is probably not entirely true on Juan's part. He had to have known the reason given for dismissal wasn't a lack of work. The Tenant Improvement Department had more work than they could handle at the time."

"What did he think the real reason was?"

"According to what Juan told me after his dismissal by Neal, there was a vague reference to tools missing during their conversation. Neal asked Juan if he had any idea who was responsible but Juan had no clue. Neal didn't pursue the topic any further, but the implication had been made."

"You mean Neal thought Juan was responsible?"

"That's what Juan was afraid of. But next thing he knew, Neal was thanking him for the work he had done for the company and handing him a letter of recommendation. Juan didn't ask outright if Neal thought he was guilty. He needed a job badly so he wasn't about to risk losing a good reference."

"You mean he might have been shooting himself in the foot if he had attempted to learn the real cause for his termination."

"Exactly. Besides giving him the reference, Neal suggested another building company where Juan could apply for employment. He told Juan to have the company call him and he would be happy to confirm the reference he had given Juan."

"Whole thing sounds pretty confusing for Juan."

"It was. After Juan was dismissed, there were no more occurrences of missing inventory. Juan's direct supervisor never felt Juan was responsible and would have liked to clear any doubts about Juan. Unfortunately, it was easier for everyone to let the matter drop rather than incur Neal's displeasure by investigating further."

"It sounds like Neal may have had an ulterior motive in terminating Juan."

"I thought so at the time. But if that was true, I never figured out what Neal was up to."

"Speaking of thefts, was your company ever hit by the Construction Site Burglars?

"Yes, but we were lucky. A forklift was stolen from one of our sites. But Neal asked me to review the insurance coverage on all of our equipment the week before the theft so our loss was fully covered when it happened."

"Fortuitous timing on Neal's part," Tom suggested, skepticism registering in his voice. He didn't believe in anything happening by accident or chance when it came to crime.

"Yes, it was, wasn't it?" Amanda lowered her head, deep in thought.

Tom gave her a moment to consider what she had told him, wondering if she would see the connection in the sequence of events.

"Let's get to the purpose of my visit." Tom pulled a picture from his shirt pocket. "This appears to be a picture of Neal taken at a local event. First, can you tell me where this picture was taken?

"It's the annual 'Protect Our Marine Life' charity event. They hold it at the Fairgrounds by the Boardwalk to bring attention to the whales, dolphins, and other aquatic life dying or being killed because of the pollution in the ocean. This picture was taken in front of Santa Rosa Hall, the big hall equipped with a full kitchen. They can fit more than three hundred tables in the main room and they fill all the tables every year. It's a very successful event."

"There are six facilities at the Fairgrounds. How do you know this is Santa Rosa Hall and that event?"

"Neal's standing in front of his car. Look closely. Directly behind him is the entrance to the building. Attached to the large window above the door is a dolphin, the signature banner for the event."

"Good eye, Amanda. Now for a tougher question. Can you guess who the other person in the picture might be? It could have been someone saying hello, or it could have been someone he took to the event. Would his calendar indicate who he was with?"

"I don't need his calendar. I can tell you he attended the event alone. He had purchased a higher priced ticket to sit at the table with some of the city bigwigs: the Mayor, the Planning Director, and a member of the City Council. He told me he wasn't taking a date because he wouldn't have time to mix pleasure with business. Knowing Neal, he had his own agenda that night," she suggested coyly. "It wouldn't have included any concern for dolphins."

"One last question." Tom handed the folded scrap of paper to Amanda. "Any idea what these numbers are? Did Neal have an office safe, locker, or a room he kept padlocked?"

"These numbers look familiar. Give me a minute while I go check something."

Tom waited impatiently, tapping his fingers on the conference table. He knew his chances of catching the murderer decreased with each passing day. He badly needed a breakthrough in this case.

Amanda returned to the conference room beaming. "We're in luck. Those numbers are the combination for a locker in the employee gym. Neal asked me to make a note of his number in case he lost or forgot it."

Tom's jaw gaped: "The employees have a gym?"

"The entire sixth floor of this office building is a fitness center for employees and their families. Mr. Carson is a strong advocate of the theory a healthier person is a happier, more productive person. He maintains a vigorous exercise program himself and wants all of his employees to have access to the level of fitness he enjoys. The center offers free weights and machines, aerobics classes, even a kids club to entertain children while their parents work out."

"Very generous of him."

"His generosity reaps benefits. Our company has a remarkably low rate of sick days and on-the-job accidents."

"I need to see Neal's locker."

66

"I can take you down to the sixth floor and help you find it. You can stay for a workout if you like," she added with a coquettish grin. "Tone your six-pack, not that it needs toning."

"Maybe another time," he smiled. Following her from the conference room, Tom unconsciously sucked in his stomach.

He was quiet on the elevator, deep in thought. *It seems unlikely Neal's gym locker is going to reveal the incriminating evidence whoever vandalized Neal's condo seemed intent on destroying. On the other hand, there's little likelihood of that person knowing of the existence of the locker. It may, indeed, have provided safe storage.*

The weight room was deserted this time of day. Amanda informed him by six o'clock, all of the equipment would be in use and the classes filled to capacity. Making their way to the back of the men's locker room, she stopped and pointed to the largest locker on the far wall.

Tom stopped her as she reached to grasp the lock and dial the numbers: "Let me do it." He pulled on a pair of latex gloves before entering the combination.

The locker was crammed but everything was neatly organized. T-shirts were on hangers; shorts were folded on the top shelf with training shoes stacked on top of them. There were no pictures, receipts, or papers of any kind. The only other item was a large plastic bag on the bottom. Tom pulled it out, emptying the contents on the floor in front of them.

Amanda gasped: "I don't understand."

"What's wrong?"

"These are some of the tools missing from the warehouse."

"You mean the ones Neal implied Juan had taken?" Amanda didn't answer Tom's question directly. Shrugging her shoulders, she spread her hands in front of her, shaking her head.

Their discovery had dismayed Tom as well. Until the pieces began to click together.

Neal not only dismissed Juan. He himself was the instigator of the theft which became the implied reason for termination. Neal had a personal agenda in all of this, and I'm beginning to understand what it was.

Chapter Eight

Lea was turning off her computer when she got a call from Paul. "I'm meeting Tom at the Crab Shack for a beer after work. Want to join us?"

"Sure. Why don't we order a couple of buckets of shrimp and crab and that can be our dinner? I'll tell Jon to have Michael over after basketball practice. They can order a pizza."

"Great. See you at the Shack at 6:00." Paul had an afterthought before ending the call. "Lea, I have things to tell Tom about the murder, but it's not an invitation for you to start asking questions."

"Of course not," she agreed, crossing her fingers. "But give. What goodies have you come up with?"

"I had to interview someone today about the burglaries and took the opportunity to eliminate him as a suspect in the murder. You'll hear about it when I tell Tom."

"See you soon, sweetheart." Lea's finger jumped from the end call button to her sister's number. "Paul and I are meeting Tom at the Crab Shack for a drink and eats. Think up a pretense to meet us there and we can get the latest on the burglaries and the murder."

"I don't need an excuse. I'm planning to stop by several restaurants tonight to drop off posters. I'm asking owners to display the posters for the 'Food and Music under the Stars' Fundraiser next month."

"Great cover. As a heads up, Paul already cautioned me about not getting involved."

"Then I guess I'll have to be the one to pry information out of our illustrious Detective."

"Tom's never been able to resist you. Just bat your long lashes and crinkle your cute button nose. He'll tell you everything he knows."

Maddy's laugh was infectious. "Oh, yeah. I'm so irresistible to Tom he's never seen me as more than a friend."

"You're the one who draws that line, Sis, ever since your divorce. You only let a man get so close before you shut him out."

"Oh, oh. This conversation sounds familiar. Gotta run, Lea. See you at six."

Lea ended the call shaking her head. *In ways, I hope my sister finds another good relationship even if she never remarries. In other ways, Maddy's one of those women who seem perfectly capable and happy living on their own, calling their own shots. Besides, I can't imagine the man who could be a match for my irrepressible sister.*

* * *

The tall wooden doors of the Crab Shack opened into a deep room with a bar along one side. Every stool was occupied. The alluring clink of glasses and ice rattling could be heard above the buzz.

The zigzag of tables on the opposite side of the room included couples and family groups. Lea and Paul sat at one of the round tables sipping beer from frosted mugs, catching up on each other's day. The smell of marinated fish cooking on the grill wafted over their heads whetting their appetites.

Lea glimpsed the hostess embraced in a hug with a tall, blond man wearing khakis and a white button-down shirt. She reached to touch Paul's arm, nodding toward the entrance. "Tom's here."

The Detective strode through the room with his usual air of calm authority, scoring attention from the waitresses with the kind of good looks that stop people in their tracks. Muscles rippled across every part of his well-toned physique but Lea knew he took care of his body more for his job than from a sense of vanity.

Nodding and smiling at people along the way, he exuded coolness and quiet self-possession.

Lea waved to get his attention. "It's no wonder he's considered the second most eligible bachelor in town."

"With the passing of Neal Henderson, he's probably been elevated to the top spot now," Paul pointed out.

Lea winced. "Don't remind him. You know how he hates any kind of public attention."

Paul raised his mug in a salute as his friend eased his lanky frame onto one of four tall bar stools. "Hey, buddy; just in time. We're getting ready to order a couple of buckets of fish."

"Sounds great. I'm hungry enough to eat a horse."

"In that case," Lea laughed, "we'll double the order."

"Bring me a beer, please, Sue," Tom told the waitress who approached their table. "No, go ahead and make it two."

They were discussing softball league standings and the latest fires in the northern part of the state when Lea stood abruptly, waving her arm above her head. "Look who's at the front desk."

Paul and Tom swiveled their chairs to watch Maddy handing a stack of posters to the restaurant manager. Looking casually around the room, Maddy noted Lea's frantic waving and headed in their direction.

She floated across the room, swaying her hips like a runway model. With a voluptuous figure and legs which seemed to go on forever, she attracted her own share of attention. She plopped onto the remaining bar stool Lea held out for her.

"Look who the cat dragged in," Paul commented, staring daggers at his wife.

"Hey, Maddy, how's everything?" Tom leaned over to give her a peck on the cheek.

"Great, Tom, how's yourself?"

"You know my job. I'm either throwing swish balls at the basketball hoop in my office going stir crazy, or I'm buried, no pun intended, in dead bodies and burglaries like I am now."

"The whole town's talking, Tom. Making any progress?" Lea let the question slip out casually. Squirming uncomfortably under her husband's heated glare, she refused to meet his gaze turning her attention to the beer Sue poured in front of her.

"Actually, there has been a development. As likely as it seemed initially, we're reasonably certain now the burglaries and the murder weren't committed by the same person or persons. There may be a connection between the two acts, but there's more than one perpetrator."

Paul took a hot roll from the basket Sue placed on their table. "I'm surprised. How can you be sure?"

"We got plenty of fingerprints from the van. You'd think they would have worn gloves, but it's not the first time I've given burglars more credit for smarts than they deserve."

Tom leaned back in his chair, savoring the buttered roll he popped in his mouth. "The body was a different matter entirely. No prints anywhere. Considering the carelessness in dealing with the van, there should have been. Plus, the footprints didn't match. We discerned three different sets of footprints around the van and leading to a spot approximately three feet from the body. Footprints near the body had been hastily covered with sand but the partial print remaining told us there was a fourth person."

Paul raised his empty bottle, gesturing to Sue to bring another round of beers to the table. "Were you able to trace the fingerprints found in the van?"

"Oh, yeah. We've put out an APB for the suspects. They're local Hispanics."

Paul's heart skipped a beat waiting for Tom to continue. "Three brothers, the oldest released from prison recently. He was sent up on similar charges. Guess he didn't learn how to stay out of trouble while he was doing time."

Maddy's eyes widened. "Wow, we were at the donut shop yesterday morning and . . ."

Paul jerked his head, cutting a quick, curious look at Lea. Her hand flew out to grab Maddy's necklace: "Maddy, you didn't tell me you went ahead and bought this necklace. I love it on you." Looking at the two men, she put her hand to her mouth. "Oops. Sorry, guys. Didn't mean to interrupt. What were you saying about the donut shop, Maddy?" She looked pleadingly at her sister.

"I was saying I had two chocolate donuts so no dessert for me." She fingered the dessert menu in the napkin holder, as Lea expelled the breath she was holding.

Returning to Tom's story, Lea didn't hide her contempt. "And now the oldest brother is getting his younger brothers in trouble, willing to let them suffer the same fate?"

"Not exactly a good role model, huh?" Tom's eyes narrowed as he turned to Paul. "Until we found their prints, they weren't on our suspect list for the burglaries. In fact, from an anonymous tip we received, your client's employee was at the top of the list." Tom leaned back, arms folded across his chest. "Fingering . . . or should I say fingerprinting . . . the brothers lets your client's employee off the hook for those burglaries. But your client didn't know about the anonymous tip we received so what made him suspicious of Juan Martinez in the first place?"

"My client had a tip of his own. His site manager found a note taped to the door of the construction trailer suggesting Juan as someone they should look into. Jim asked me to intervene as a neutral third party to determine any possible involvement on Juan's part." Paul signaled the waitress, pointing at the bread basket for a refill. "After interviewing Juan, I completely eliminated the possibility of his involvement in my own mind, but I'm glad your findings have confirmed my judgment."

Lea nudged Paul's shoulder. "You've always been a good judge of people, sweetheart."

73

Tom lifted a beer to his lips, draining the bottle. His next comment took his listeners by surprise. "Actually, the fact Neal was apparently meeting the brothers gives us reason to believe Neal himself was the mastermind."

Paul's face registered shock. "What motive would Neal have to be involved in something so underhanded? From my dealings with Don Carson's company, I've seen he treats his employees generously. Surely, Neal's salary was more than enough to support even his lavish lifestyle."

"You'd think, wouldn't you? I mean, how much does a single guy need to live comfortably in this small town?" Paul had obviously touched a nerve involving Tom's pay as a public official.

"It turns out Neal was behind schedule and over budget on several of Don's projects," Tom explained. "His poor management of those jobs was threatening to tarnish Don's reputation as well as significantly reduce the developer's net worth. From what Ken Crosby told me this morning, Neal was pouring his own money into the projects to keep Don from finding out what a bad job he was doing."

"Do you think he was worried about Don firing him?"

"Probably. It's common knowledge Don thought of Neal as a second son. But common wisdom also has it Don's going to pass his business on to his son when he retires, regardless of whether or not his son chooses to be involved in it. He would never tolerate his legacy being diminished before that event occurs."

"I still don't see what led Neal to become involved in the burglaries," Maddy interjected.

"We examined his financial records after his death. It was obvious from credit card and bank statements he was living way beyond his means. He'd already been drawing more than his salary from the projects. When they went over budget, he needed money to pump back in to stop the cash flow hemorrhage. He turned to an illegal source of cash . . . the sale of stolen goods

74

across the border. Construction materials were the obvious choice to steal because he had the knowledge and contacts in the business to pull it off."

"How did he obtain knowledge of the construction sites?"

"During their high school years, Neal and Don's son spent their summers working for almost every builder in the County learning the business. He either had information first hand or was privy to everything he needed to organize a team of thugs and instruct them explicitly on how to carry out the thefts."

Lea shook her head as she pushed her empty plate to the side. "Wow, he was a pretty cool customer, working every day in an industry he was robbing blind at night. How is his family taking all this? Did you tell them of your suspicion Neal was complicit in the burglaries?"

"Not yet. I didn't feel a need to add to their burden at this early stage of the investigation. I was the one to notify the father of his son's death. From the brief conversation we had, Neal and his father had barely talked in recent weeks. His second wife, Neal's stepmother, had nothing to offer. She was clearly more concerned with her husband's reaction to Neal's death than Neal's death itself. I may talk with the father after he's recovered from the shock, but I don't get the impression he was privy to Neal's private life. I'm interviewing the sister tomorrow. Maybe she'll know more about his current activities."

Paul brought his attention back to Tom's allegation. "If you believe Neal was behind the burglaries, doesn't that suggest he may have been the one who provided the anonymous tip about Juan to divert suspicion from himself? And from the two brothers who were working on the construction site which was burglarized?"

"Seems to be the logical conclusion. We may be able to prove it when we get phone records from Neal's office. A call to the police station and a subsequent call to Jim's site manager would certainly indicate he was the tipster."

"Maybe Neal arranged to have the brothers steal small equipment from his own site to set Juan up as a viable suspect for the burglaries," Paul theorized, leaning his elbows on the table. "He only needed to keep suspicion off himself and his activities long enough to finish the projects he was working on for Don. Once they started pre-selling, his cash flow problems would be over, and the burglaries could mysteriously stop."

Tom nodded, continuing the supposition. "Neal had probably instructed the brothers to drive the stolen goods directly from the heist to the border. The meeting at the Pier could have been their payoff from Neal before heading out of the County. Henderson may have already made long-term arrangements for the brothers to stay in Mexico to make sure neither they nor he, were ever tied to the burglaries."

"If your theory about Neal is correct, you've got the burglaries pretty well figured out. That leaves the murder," Maddy prodded. "But Neal being the mastermind also rules out a motive for the brothers to kill him."

"Unless the meeting at the pier erupted into a spontaneous confrontation," Lea suggested.

Tom rubbed the back of his neck, twisting his head in both directions. "The time of death tells us Neal was already dead by the time the brothers got to the meet. The most likely scenario is they found his body under the Pier, panicked, and fled the scene, abandoning the truck."

Lea's eyes narrowed. "Which leads you back to the extra set of prints where the body was found . . . the fourth person."

Paul dropped a credit card on top of the bill tray and handed the tray to Sue. "The fourth person being someone who knew Neal would be at the Pier waiting for the van?"

"Exactly," Tom agreed. "Killing Neal at the Pier would provide a perfect trail to place the blame on the brothers. It would look like what we originally suspected: a meet gone wrong, maybe an argument over the amount Neal paid them. It gave the

76

killer the opportunity to create evidence directly linking the brothers."

Maddy raised a finger. "But you said the brothers' footprints were only in the sand next to the parking lot, not where the body was found under the Pier."

"That's the catch. We figure the killer's timing went wrong. He, or she, planned to kill Neal after the brothers left so there would be plenty of footprints and evidence of their meeting. But the murderer ended up killing Neal before the van arrived. Maybe Neal recognized the person and confronted him. Maybe the murderer panicked when the van didn't arrive on time and decided to go ahead and carry out his plan to get rid of Neal. It's one of those mistakes which occur in every murder. Something happens the murderer doesn't anticipate. Something that later provides us with the clues we need to recreate actual events. In this case, it helped us decipher there were different perpetrators in two separate crimes instead of the same perpetrators for both crimes."

"So the killer is still at large."

"Yep. He, or she, is still out there, thinking they got away with it." Standing, Tom stretched his legs and grabbed his baseball cap. "It's time for me to get back to work to see if I can flush them out. Talk to you guys later. Good to see you, Maddy."

"You, too, Tom," Maddy smiled. "Be careful and stay safe."

After Tom's departure, Paul turned to the women. "Why am I feeling you two are more involved in these crimes than you should be? You haven't been putting your noses in places they don't belong, have you?"

"Paul, you give us no credit," Maddy objected, winking at Lea. "We may like the occasional bout of harmless sleuthing, but we'd never be foolish enough to put ourselves in real danger by interjecting ourselves into crimes as serious as these. Gotta run. Call you tomorrow, Sis." She grabbed her posters and made a hasty exit before Paul could ask more questions.

It would be less than a matter of hours before Maddy would be wishing the denial she proffered her brother-in-law had been true.

* * *

Paul and Lea pulled into their driveway as Lea's cell phone buzzed, indicating her sister was calling. "Locked yourself out again?"

"No, but if Paul's listening, you can use that as an excuse for why I'm calling. When Tom mentioned his interview with Neal's father, a bell went off. Tom said the stepmother didn't offer him much information, but I know the woman. She loves to gossip. She'd be more than happy to tell us everything she knows about Neal."

Lea hesitated, thinking of a response which wouldn't alarm Paul. "You wouldn't have taken your house key out of your purse at the restaurant so it's either still in your purse or in your car."

Maddy understood Lea's response. "I'll call Liz tomorrow and tell her I have new dining room pieces I think she'd be interested in. After I've shown her the display on the floor room, I'll invite her for a latte at the Starbucks next door. You can run into us and say you were shopping at the fabric store in the center."

Paul glanced suspiciously in Lea's direction as he pressed the garage door opener. She knew she needed to end the conversation. "Just use your spare key under the flower pot and look for your house key tomorrow when you can see what you're doing."

"We'll be sitting at a table in front of Starbucks at one-thirty. Meet us there."

"Oh, good, I'm glad you found it."

She shook her head for Paul's benefit. "Maddy would lose her head if it weren't permanently attached."

Later the same night, Lea took Gracie to the back yard to do her business before settling in. "I don't like being elusive with Paul, girl, but I think sometimes he's overly protective. What Maddy and I do is perfectly harmless and you never know when we might discover useful information. I agree with Maddy. Liz is more likely to open up to us in private than to anyone representing the heavy hand of the law. Besides, I think she'll be more candid about her son-in-law when Neal's father isn't around to hear her remarks."

Gracie looked at Lea, listening intently to every word. She wagged her tail in anticipation of the coming day's events.

Chapter Nine

Maddy sang along with her favorite Country Western radio station as she drove the sisters to her dentist appointment.

"How can you be so chipper when you're going to the dentist?" Lea asked.

"You're the one afraid of dentists, not me."

Lea shrugged her shoulders. "I'll be the first to admit to being a dental coward. I'm also not crazy about flying. You, like Mom, are fearless when it comes to almost everything."

Maddy shook her hair smiling broadly as she pulled into the underground parking at the medical building which housed her dentist. "I only hope you can get enough information to eliminate Beth as a suspect. I haven't heard any reports of her being interviewed by the police. But anyone who knows about her being rebuffed at the altar can't help but wonder if the emotional pain of that mortifying situation caught up with her and made her do something irrational."

"If Neal Henderson would have come out at the time with a reason for calling off the wedding, it could have made the situation a whole lot more bearable. But from the rumors circulating, Beth was as much in the dark as everyone else as to why Neal changed his mind. It left room for a lot of speculation, most of which was unfavorable to Beth."

Maddy scoffed. "I thought she was well rid of the jerk. At least now, he'll never be in a position to cause her further embarrassment."

"Hmmm," Lea mused, opening the door to the dentist's office. "Are we talking about motive now?"

Stepping into the reception area, she was glad to see there was no one else in the room so talking with Beth would be easier. After greetings were exchanged, Beth signaled Maddy to go through to the hygienist's room.

Lea couldn't help but notice Beth's red eyes as the distressed woman folded a tissue and dabbed her nose. Obviously, Beth hadn't had enough time to recover from what she was feeling.

"I'm so sorry for what you must be going through, Beth," Lea commiserated. "It must have been a terrible shock."

Lea could see Beth was struggling to maintain her composure but her tone came off callous and unsympathetic. "For someone to be murdered at his age; of course, it's unfathomable. Those things just don't happen in this small town. I can't imagine why anyone would have done such a deplorable thing." Busying herself with paperwork in front of her, she seemed anxious to close the conversation.

"Had you or Neal's other friends seen much of him lately?" Lea asked, trying to keep the tone casual.

"Neal hadn't been in touch with any of our old group for months. Apparently, his job was demanding all his time and attention."

Lea wondered if there were other distractions besides his work which had alienated Neal. She tried to give Beth an opening to denigrate her former fiancé: "Neal's fast rise up the ranks in Don Carson's company was probably quite a game changer for him. It was hard not to notice the flashy red sports cars he was driving around town."

At that moment, Maddy returned to the reception area in time to hear the vitriolic comment which took both her and her sister by surprise.

"Neal got all the goodies he was after. Too bad, he won't be able to enjoy them."

* * *

Tom arranged to meet Neal's sister, Joan Mannix, at a coffee shop close to the hospital where she was an RN. She had made it clear she could give him only thirty minutes of her time since they were short handed on her shift.

He had no problem recognizing her when he walked into Mel's Diner. The woman sitting alone at a table next to the front window was remarkably similar in looks to her late brother. The same blond hair pulled back from a wide forehead, the high cheekbones, and the piercing hazel eyes which met his greeting.

Sliding into the booth across from her, he signaled the waitress for coffee. "I appreciate your taking the time to see me here. I know what hospitals are like. I was afraid we wouldn't be able to have much of a conversation there without you getting a lot of interruptions."

"You're right." She shook her head, pouring cream into her coffee. "It's typically pretty chaotic but I'm used to it. It's actually nice for me to get a breather like this. It's rare I'm able to take a break during my shift."

"Do you work twelve-hour shifts?"

"No. I'm in the minority at Buena General, working an eight-hour shift. I worked twelve-hour shifts before we started a family. When our son was born, I took a year off to be at home. I requested eight-hour shifts when I went back to work. Then our daughter came along two years later so I made the switch to shorter shifts permanent.

I almost went back to twelve-hour shifts when the kids were in elementary school. There was a high demand and a shortage of nurses at the hospital. But I made our family my priority and I've never regretted my decision. Both kids are in middle school now, and believe me; they need quite a bit of supervision. I can't imagine what high school will be like. They're both good kids but high school can be a trying time for any young person."

Tom sympathized. "Not having kids of my own, I lack your experience with that side of adolescence. But in my line of work, I

82

see quite a bit of what happens when parents aren't there for their kids. I think you made the right decision."

A smile crossed Joan's face. "Thank you for saying that. I'm lucky to have a husband who helps with the children, but he's an attorney so he works longer hours than I do."

"Mannix. Is your husband the Mannix of Johnston, Mannix, and Watkins?"

"Yes, that's Bob. I'm just grateful his firm practices corporate law. At least he's not typically tied up in litigation involving a lot of court appearances."

Tom smiled. "Regrettably, I probably spend more time in court than your husband does."

"Which begs the question of why you're taking the time to see me. What is it I can help you with? I imagine you're here to ask about my brother."

"I'm sorry for your family's loss. I know these are difficult days for you."

"Losing someone at a young age is hard for any family. My mother would have taken Neal's death the hardest, but she passed when Neal and I were young. Her battle with cancer was one of the things which led me into the nursing profession."

"Where you close to your brother?"

"Not very. I'm six years older than my brother so we were never together in school."

"What about Neal and your father?"

She paused, choosing her words carefully. "My father and Neal have never been terribly close. I'd have to say I've always been Dad's favorite.

Those two never saw eye-to-eye. Growing up, arguments between the two of them were common in our house. My mother was the peacekeeper. I went to my room to study any time the shouting started. It may have been a factor leading to my high grades in school." Her remarks were self-effacing but to the point.

"How was it when your father remarried?"

83

She stared into her coffee cup. "It was great by me. I was glad to see him happy again. But my stepmother never got along particularly well with Neal. She felt he took advantage of Dad."

"In what way?"

"Neal has always been careless with money. Even as a kid, he spent all of his allowance as soon as he got it. Never saved a nickel. Ever since he graduated college, he's had grandiose delusions about himself and how he's meant to live. As far back as I can remember, he's maintained a lavish lifestyle. Usually beyond his salary level. Anytime there was a shortfall, he had no qualms about asking Dad for money to tide him over. Money never repaid, to my knowledge."

From her clipped tone, it was obvious to Tom there was no love lost between the siblings.

"Did you see a lot of your brother?"

"On special occasions but otherwise infrequently. We always had the family to our house for holiday dinners. Last year, he brought his fiancé for Thanksgiving and Christmas. As almost everyone in town knows, he broke the relationship off in an ignominious fashion. To be honest, the way he basically jilted Beth Owens at the altar didn't surprise me. I'm actually glad, for Beth's sake. She probably didn't feel that way at the time but she was better off without him."

"Do you think Beth harbored resentment against your brother for the way he embarrassed her?"

"She would have had every right to, but no. Beth isn't that kind of person. She was more likely to blame herself. I'm sure it was a matter of my brother being enticed to what he perceived as bigger and better things."

"Can you be more specific?"

"Not really. But after Christmas dinner, Neal was in the kitchen fixing himself a drink while I got the desserts ready. I asked him how he felt about his upcoming nuptials. He seemed even more cavalier than usual. Threw off a sarcastic comment about his not being cut out for monogamy. I asked what he meant. He laughed, picked up his drink, and walked out to the back yard to join the others. We never discussed it again."

"I'm not implying anything in particular, but I have to ask. Do you know if Neal had any enemies?"

"Don't worry about hurting my feelings. I've never been protective of my brother's reputation like our father has. I believe everyone earns their reputation through their actions."

Joan lowered her head, folding her hands in her lap. "The way Neal acted, I'm sure there were plenty of people who didn't like him. There were undoubtedly people besides Beth whom he treated unfairly or badly."

She raised her head and looked directly at Tom. "But we weren't involved in each other's lives enough so I can shed any light on anyone who hated my brother enough to kill him."

The candor of the statement caught in her throat. For the first time, Tom saw pain reflected in her eyes.

He extended his hand across the table to drop a business card beside her cup. "You've been very helpful. Again, I appreciate your seeing me at this difficult time. If anything else comes to mind, or if I can be of assistance to you or your family, please don't hesitate to call me."

He picked up the bill, walking Joan to the front door of the diner before returning to the cash register to pay. Pulling money from his wallet, he saw her talking on her cell phone even before she crossed the street to return to the hospital.

* * *

Lea arrived early at the shopping center where Maddy's furniture store was located, giving herself time to park and go into the fabric store well before Maddy and Liz would arrive at Starbucks. "At least I won't be deceitful telling them where I've been," she told herself.

After buying a skein of yarn, Sherlock's favorite thing to play with, she walked in the direction of Starbucks. Being careful not to slow down as she walked by the coffee store, she listened for her name to be called.

"Lea, hey, Lea."

Turning, the smiled at the two women sitting at the front table.

"Hi, Maddy. I was at the fabric store. Decided to pop by to see if you could take a coffee break with me."

"Perfect timing. I'm on my break now." Turning to the woman sitting across from her, she made introductions. Liz Henderson was a middle-aged, petite woman with short gray layered hair and tastefully applied makeup.

"Please join us." Liz indicated an empty chair at their table.

"Thank you. I'd love to. Missed my morning coffee before my day got started. An iced latte will hit the spot."

When Lea returned to the table after receiving her drink, Maddy was deep in conversation with Liz. "How is Harold doing? It must have been a terrible shock for him."

"He's getting better. Our doctor gave him a prescription which has helped him sleep the last several nights. Of course, the funeral was terrible but things are getting back to normal if there can ever be such a thing as normal again. Frankly, I'm glad you called. I needed to get away from the house and away from Harold's brooding for a couple of hours."

"Were Neal and Harold close?"

"Not really. Joan is the one who takes after Harold. They've always had a close relationship. Harold would never admit he wasn't close to his son, but it's the truth. Neal was a hard person for anyone to get close to. I don't mean to discredit Neal but he was an extremely self-centered individual." Her eyebrows formed a crease as her lips pursed. "I'm not sure he cared for anyone except himself."

"Someone else gave nearly the same description of Neal when they described the way he broke off with his fiancé."

Liz made no effort to hide her feelings. "The way he handled the whole despicable affair was unforgivable. I'm not saying he should have gone through with a marriage he had reason to believe wouldn't last, but the manner in which he humiliated that girl was reprehensible."

Lea could see Liz Henderson was quite an outspoken force and could easily imagine how she and Neal may have butted heads.

"Did Neal ever discuss his business affairs with his father and you?"

"Never. That was one of his biggest problems. He felt he didn't need anyone's help or advice. From the first time I met the young man, he struck me as the type who thought he was smarter than everybody else. He was the expert. A know-it-all. I think he viewed asking for guidance as a sign of weakness.

Harold told me in his middle and high school years, Neal never asked his parents for help with his homework. He never had study buddies over to work on projects together. Neal wanted to do things on his own so when he got a good grade, he could take full credit. It was the reason he chose track and tennis. Because those weren't team sports."

"Was he good in sports?"

"He excelled. And when he won, he took all the glory. He didn't have to share it with teammates."

Liz folded and refolded the napkin beside her coffee cup as she spoke. Lea wondered if it was still the strain of the week's events.

"No, he never came to Harold asking for advice or discussing his job. But he was more than willing to come to his father when he needed a little something to tide him over between paychecks or when he overextended his credit lines. Harold was always willing to open his checkbook for Neal. I think it made him feel useful; like he had something to offer his son. Of course, the so-called loans were hardly loans because they were never repaid but Harold didn't seem to mind."

"Did you notice your son-in-law acting differently in any way lately?"

Liz hesitated, placing her elbows on the arms of the chair and tilting her hands in a pyramid under her chin. "As a matter of fact, I did think something was going on with Neal the last several weeks. Something other than the negative feedback he was getting for the way he ended his engagement."

"What made you think so?"

"He called one evening late. We had listened to the news and were ready for bed. Harold and Neal had a brief conversation. It finished abruptly and Harold was visibly upset. When I asked him about it, he was reluctant to share the details. Neal was still at work, apparently worried about something to do with one of his projects. Harold was asking how he could help when Neal interrupted to say someone was coming into his office. He told his father to disregard the call. He would work it out and didn't need any help."

"Did he hear any more about it from Neal?"

"Not a word. My husband called Neal several times the next day but the calls went to voice mail each time. Harold started to worry something might have happened to Neal but he finally got a call back around dinnertime. Neal sounded happy and relaxed. Told his father everything was fine and he was on his way to a concert. It's the last time Harold spoke to Neal before. . ." Liz choked, her eyes tearing. "Not a meaningful exchange for a final conversation with his son."

Maddy reached across the table placing her hands over those of the distraught woman to quiet the fingers folding and unfolding the napkin. "It will take time, dear, but Harold has you and Joan."

"I should get back to him now. Let's go to the store so I can get my car." Turning to Lea, she apologized. "Sorry, I'm not myself today but hopefully, we'll see each other again soon under better circumstances."

"Of course," Lea responded, retrieving her package as she stood. "Talk to you tomorrow, Maddy."

Watching the two women walk away, Lea reflected: *Does Tom know about the late hour visitor to Neal's office the night before he was murdered? Had that person offered a resolution to Neal's problem, the source of Neal's good mood the next day?*

She considered the bigger question. *How can I pass this information on to Tom without Paul finding out what Maddy and I have been up to?*

Chapter Ten

Tom was at his desk when a call from the Chief of Police was patched through to him. The smile on his face told the other detectives it was good news. He called them over to his desk. "They caught two of the brothers at the entrance to the border crossing. I called a couple of days ago to confirm the border patrol had received the APB on the brothers since Mexico was their most likely destination. Sure enough, they showed up ready to walk across the border and the authorities took them into custody."

He pointed out two officers leaning against the wall. "Nelson and Jones in the Burglary Unit are going to get them and bring them back here, but we'll get a crack at them in interrogation to find out what they know about the Henderson murder."

"Where's the third brother?"

"The brothers weren't cooperating with the officers who detained them but initial questioning indicates he never left the County. He told his brothers not to worry; he'd get his hands on money and anything else they needed, and meet them in Mexico. The other supplies he mentioned may refer to weapons so we need to include an armed and dangerous alert on the APB."

"Any ideas on where he's headed for money and supplies, sir?"

"I want to make sure we cover all the bases. I've divided the Unit into pairs covering all the possible places he might go. You can get your assignments on the way out.

One team will go to the last known address where the brothers were living and visit their family. Another team will check with the brother's parole officer to determine when that officer last had contact with Roberto. Be sure to get any addresses and contact numbers the parole board has on file. I'll go back to the vic's office and condominium in case the brother left something in Neal's possession he wants to retrieve."

Tom walked briskly toward the door. "Hopefully, the APB will result in the third brother's arrest before the day's over. If not, let's meet back here before the end of shift to coordinate our findings. Stay safe out there. Remember, this guy could be armed by now. He's headed back to prison once he's caught so he's got nothing to lose."

* * *

Maddy was scheduled for the evening hours at the furniture store. She had plenty of time for an aerobics class after her dental appointment.

"I shouldn't stop at Maria's on the way. Her donuts will offset all my hard work at class. On the other hand," she rationalized, "a little reward is good motivation."

Entering the shop, she encountered a visibly distraught Maria muttering under her breath as she put a tray of pastry dough into the oven.

"Maria, you look angry. What's wrong?"

"I've got no patience with men who show no respect," she explained, waving her hands in the air.

"Who's been showing you no respect?"

"Roberto Ramirez came in this morning and he sure wasn't here to buy no donuts. He was ranting about how his brother Miguel saw me talking to the police. He wanted to know why the police came around and what I told them. I asked him why he was so worried about the police. Then I told him what I said or didn't say was none of his business."

"Wow. Did that make him mad?"

91

"You bet," she grinned, "but that bad temper of his has never scared me. He wanted to know if the cops asked about him and his brothers. Or if I told the cops where they live."

"Did they? And did you?" Maddy asked, breathlessly.

"I don't even know where the brothers live. That's what I told Roberto. Those boys have shifted from one place to another ever since their uncle kicked them out when he discovered they were selling drugs."

"Maria, do you know the police are looking for all three of the brothers? They're suspected of being the ones who have been doing all the burglaries. There was a blurb on the news last night saying anyone having any information about them should call the police but to avoid contact with them at all costs."

Maria's eyes widened and she swallowed hard. "I never have time to watch the news. Maybe I shouldn't have been so cheeky with Roberto. Should I call the police?"

"Yes, right away. I've got to go." Maddy hurried toward the door. "Call the police now, Maria."

"Don't you want a donut?"

"No time. I'll come by tomorrow."

Maddy felt guilty skipping her exercise class but she had other plans. Hitting a number on her cell phone, she waited impatiently for Lea to answer. Relieved the call hadn't gone to voice mail, Maddy broke in before Lea could say hello. "He's in town."

"Who's in town? What are you talking about?"

"The oldest of the burglary brothers. The one who got out of prison. I know Tom told Paul he thought the brothers were headed for Mexico but I was just at Maria's. Roberto was in her shop earlier this morning."

"What were you doing in the donut shop?" Lea interrupted. "I thought you gave up sweets."

"Never mind about that." Then, as if she was stating the obvious: "We've got to do something."

"Whoa, what do you mean we've got to do something? Maria's the only one who needs to do something. She needs to call the police right away and tell them exactly what Roberto said."

"I know, I know. She's probably on the phone to them already, but Tom's got his hands full with everything else. We could at least take a drive by the place where the brothers are staying to see if Roberto is around."

"Are you crazy?" Lea responded incredulously. "Didn't you pay attention to the newscast last night? The brothers are considered to be possibly armed and dangerous. Besides, no one knows their whereabouts or the police would have arrested them already."

"I'm sure Roberto wouldn't be crazy enough to go back to where he and his brothers were holed up, although he does sound more than a little crazy. But if we could eliminate that spot for Tom, he wouldn't have to use his resources checking it out."

"There's still the problem of not knowing where the brothers are."

"Actually, that's not a problem. Maria told Roberto she didn't tell the police where he lives because she doesn't know, but she wasn't being entirely truthful."

"Oh, oh. I don't like the sound of this."

"You remember the rancher we met at Maria's. The good looking one who looks like a model for Stetson hats?"

"The one Maria called Scott."

"He told Maria the Ramirez brothers may have been camped in the flat area of land next to the river which flooded last year when we had the heavy rains."

"How does he know?"

"The flat land is adjacent to his property. He scouts the property to make sure partying teenagers or drug addicts haven't left food to attract coyotes or other animals that cross onto his property. He saw tents that were obviously for more than overnighters. He hasn't reported it to the police because he hasn't seen any sign of the black Ford truck the Ramirez brothers drive. He'd recognize the truck if it had been there. The brothers painted red flames on it to make it stand out."

"If they're driving a truck painted with red flames, it will stand out to the officers responding to the APB, too."

"That's what I'm thinking. I told Maria to get hold of the rancher to make sure he calls the police with the information about the campsite and the truck if he hasn't already. In the meantime, I think we should drive by the campsite to see if they're still there."

"Don't bother. Paul got off the phone with Tom half an hour ago. They caught two of the brothers at the border. The only brother still on the loose is Roberto. You said Maria is calling the police about his visit today. Given the information the rancher supplies about the campsite, the police will be sure to check it out."

Lea's reasoning skills surfaced. "Besides, it seems unlikely Roberto would have reason to return to the campsite with his brothers gone. It sounds like he's after something other than their camping supplies. It's doubtful they would have left money at a campsite. He must have a different target in mind."

In the ensuing silence, Lea could almost hear Maddy's brain churning. She was relieved to hear her sister concur with her reasoning. "You're right, Lea. It's none of our business. If I hurry, I'll still make my exercise class. Talk to you later."

Lea was right, she thought. But looking at her watch, she elected to follow her own intuition. *There's no way I can get to class on time. The instructor hates it when someone disrupts the warm-up routine by walking in late. Missing class gives me more than enough time to take a little detour before I have to go to work. I'll just take the long way home by driving past the river instead of on the freeway.*

Maddy exited the freeway onto the unpaved frontage road that ran along the river. The river carried water from the mountains all the way to the ocean after flowing across the plains, making them fertile with silt and providing the basis for the rich agriculture of the area. There were few homes in this area because of the likelihood of flooding from the river during the rainy season, but flooding was of no concern to Maddy at this time of year. Typically bare through early spring, the river bed itself was only now beginning to show signs of vegetation.

Not far from the exit, Maddy passed the RV campground. She observed a few spots occupied but in another month, the entire campground would be full and booked through the summer.

As the road narrowed, she was surrounded on either side by large groves of willows, cottonwoods, and alders, ideal spots for picnics or camping. Springtime rendered perfect weather for camping increasing Maddy's hopes of finding signs the brothers had a campsite along the river.

Lowering her window as she drove past thickets of wild rose and blackberry, she heard the warbling of multiple bird species common to the area. But it was the sounds of campers she was listening for.

Her hopes diminished as she realized she was getting closer to the State Park. It was unlikely the brothers would have stayed there since they would be required to register, furnish identification, and pay daily fees.

She was contenting herself with a 'nothing ventured, nothing gained' attitude when she spotted it. A black truck with trailing red and orange flames painted on the side.

It was parked under a huge oak tree next to a wooden picnic table at the top of the riverbank. There were no tents or other camping paraphernalia visible but a nearby grove of willow trees could be shielding a campsite. She turned onto the graveled road leading to the picnic table to get a better look.

Won't Lea be surprised? Not only have I probably found the brothers' campsite but Roberto could be at the camp this very moment. Dialing Lea's number, she muttered. *Darn it. I'm not getting cell phone reception; I must be out of the coverage area. I'll have to drive back closer to town until I can get a signal.*

Before turning around to return to the frontage road, Maddy decided to snap a couple of pictures. *I'll email these to the police so they can pinpoint the exact location.*

She stepped out of her car and studied her cell phone, trying to adjust it to camera mode. The unexpected sound of a gruff male voice caused her to jump. "Bird watching, Miss?"

The words sent shivers along the fine hairs on her arms and the back of her neck. Turning abruptly, Maddy knew she was looking into the eyes of none other than Roberto Ramirez.

There was no question the man standing in front of her was the older brother of the two men she and Lea had seen at Maria's donut shop. He had the same dark hair, black goatee and mustache, and tattoos covering his arms from neck to wrists. A scar in the pattern of tiny railroad tracks jagged from the tip of his right ear down his cheek to the corner of his mouth. This older version of the Ramirez boys was more muscular. There were age lines etched in his face. *Maybe from hard time in prison*, Maddy thought.

She quickly collected her thoughts, hoping her voice wouldn't reflect the terror she was feeling. "Oh, hi. I'm looking for a great spot for a picnic. My family is having a reunion in June. They want me to find the perfect place. If I don't take pictures and label the different locations I'm scouting, I can't remember which spots I like best. Have you camped around here? Can you recommend something?"

Roberto scanned the woman's face suspiciously. "No, I come here to do a little fishing. How did you find this spot? It's pretty far off the freeway."

She reminded herself not to underestimate him. "The way I always find great places for a picnic. I turn my car onto a back road and go until I see something I like."

His lips drew back in a snarl. "So you're out here all alone?"

Maddy's heart skipped a beat. The palms of her hands were moist. She made a show of looking at her watch.

"I had no idea I'd been here so long. I've got to get going or I'll be late for work." She turned quickly hoping she sounded more convincing to him than she did to herself.

She was fumbling with her keys to unlock the car door when she felt a rough, hairy hand on top of hers. She trembled. He grinned broadly from ear to ear.

"You know, lady, you're about to learn the hard way you shouldn't drive back roads by yourself. So this may not be your lucky day, but it could be mine." He grabbed her cell phone, pulling her roughly down the path toward his truck. "I think I just found me a get out of town card."

Realizing his intention, Maddy knew she had to get away before he got her in his truck. Her lies had obviously not distracted him. It was time to lay out the facts.

"Hold on, Roberto. I know who you are." Her lower lip trembled but she kept her voice calm.

He twirled abruptly, towering over her. She could see the cords in his neck tighten. Clasping her hand tighter, he twisted her wrist until tears came to her eyes.

"Maybe you better tell me who you are," he demanded.

"It doesn't matter who I am," she responded tersely. "What matters is my sister Lea is on her way here right now."

Obviously relieved, he laughed scornfully. "Oh, now I'm really scared. Two women after me. I better run for my life."

Seizing her last chance before they reached the truck, Maddy threatened in a calm, low voice: "She stopped at the police station on her way to give them this exact location. You may not

97

be worried about my sister and me, but you should be worried about the full force of the Buena Viaje police force coming down on you."

The last comment got his attention but not in the way Maddy had hoped for. His face became red, distorted by rage. She screamed as he jerked her so hard she thought her arm would pull out of its socket. Her car keys fell from her hand as he pushed her in front of him.

"All you need to be worried about is what I'll do to you if you don't do what I say. We need to get out of here fast. I'll take the back roads across the mountain to the interstate. Don't try any funny business or you know what will happen to you. You're a much better hostage alive . . . but dead or alive, you're leaving town with me."

With that warning issued, Roberto pulled a roll of duct tape from the glove compartment and secured Maddy's hands behind her. "Now we're going to get on your cell phone and call your sister. Let's see if you've got her on speed dial. What's her name?"

"None of your business."

Roberto's open palm whipped across her cheek so fast and so violently she momentarily saw stars.

"Lea," Maddy whimpered.

"That's more like it," he sneered, scrolling through the numbers on her phone. "Yep, there she is."

He gave instructions, juggling her with one hand and her phone in the other. "When she answers, I'll hold the phone to your mouth. Tell her you came to the site and found nothing so the cops don't need to come out here. That's all she needs to know right now. Once we're far enough away, we'll call back to let her know you're with me and what they need to do for me to get you back."

A moment later, he raised the phone, scowling: "We're out of cell range. We'll wait until we're over the hill."

Roberto dropped the tailgate and hoisted her onto the flatbed of his truck. *At least I landed on top of the tents. They should provide a cushion from bouncing around.*

"Is this necessary?" she complained.

"There's no room for you in the front. I wasn't exactly planning on a passenger." He laughed gruffly like he was enjoying her discomfort. "But let's make sure you aren't able to make noise and attract attention back here."

Leaning over the side of the flatbed, he wrapped duct tape around her ankles and pressed a strip across her mouth. The worst part for Maddy was the dusty blanket he threw on top of her to hide her from view. *Just what I needed. The dust will set off my allergies.* She wiggled her nose, trying to stop the tickling sensation. *I've got to sneeze. Not an easy thing to do with duct tape on my mouth.*

After a last inspection of the campsite area, Roberto got into the truck and they started their journey, not toward the freeway as Maddy had hoped where there would be a greater chance of their being spotted but up the one-way back road that led over the mountain. Maddy despaired. *I'm in for a long, bumpy ride.*

* * *

Lea finished the project she was working on and emailed it with a sense of satisfaction. She stretched, looking at the border collie asleep in the middle of the room. "I'm sure my client will be satisfied with the report and will agree with my recommendations. I think we deserve a little celebration, Gracie."

Hearing her name, the dog's body rose instantly from a deep sleep. Lea laughed as Gracie raced around the desk, planting her front paws on Lea's midriff. "I'll call Maddy and see if we can take her to lunch at El Torito. I'm in the mood for Mexican food."

She dialed Maddy's cell number. Getting voice mail, Lea called the main number for the furniture store. She was told Maddy hadn't arrived for work nor had she called in. Alarm bells went off. *That's not like Maddy.*

Gracie sensed the concern in her master's voice.

"You don't think she ignored my advice and drove out to where she thought the Ramirez brothers camped, do you?"

When the dog started running in circles, Lea became more concerned. "Are you trying to tell me you think Maddy's in trouble?"

Gracie raced to the back door and began barking. "Okay, girl, we'll go see if she's at home. If she's not there, I'll call Paul. He's not going to be at all happy with us when I tell him where I think Maddy's gone, but the way you're acting tells me something's wrong. Maddy may have gotten in over her head this time."

When they arrived at Maddy's house, Gracie leaped from the car barking loudly at the front door. Lea didn't have to ring the bell to know what her sweating palms already told her. Something had happened to Maddy.

* * *

Tom was leaving the parking lot at Neal's condominium when he got the call from Paul. "I hope you're calling to tell me you want to buy me lunch. My morning has been crazy. I could use some nourishment."

"Sorry, buddy. I'm afraid your morning is about to get crazier because of my wife."

He relayed everything Lea had told him regarding what she and Maddy had learned about the Ramirez brothers.

"And now, that fool sister of Lea's has apparently gone to where Maria told her the brothers were camping. She isn't at work, she's not at home, and she's not answering her cell phone."

100

Tom detected equal parts of worry, anger, and frustration in his friend's voice.

"I've warned those two before about playing amateur sleuths. I don't know what Maddy could be thinking getting anywhere near dangerous criminals."

"Take it easy, Paul. I kind of admire Maddy's courage. She's fearless. Nothing intimidates the woman."

"Is it courage or lack of common sense?" Paul groaned.

"Oh, it's not that. Maddy is one sharp cookie. She usually knows what she's doing. She simply lacks the restrictive boundaries most people set for themselves. Wherever her intuition leads, she follows."

"This time, her intuition may have led her into the middle of a potentially volatile situation."

"I'm almost on the freeway now. I should be at the campsite in less than twenty minutes. I'll let you know what I find. In the meantime, don't be too rough on Lea. This could all amount to nothing."

"I suppose. Maybe Maddy went out last night, met someone, spent the night, and overslept this morning."

Paul was surprised at how quickly Tom disputed the suggestion.

"I doubt it. Maddy isn't seeing anyone seriously right now and she doesn't strike me as the type to spend the night with someone she barely knows."

"Since when are you an expert on her social life?"

Tom ignored the innuendo but hastened to add: "Nor is she inconsiderate or irresponsible. Even if she got a late start, it's unlikely she wouldn't have called the furniture store to let them know what time she'd be in."

"You're right," Paul conceded. "Maddy doesn't go out on hot dates or party all night. Her tastes are much more discriminating. All the more reason to be concerned about her being incommunicado now."

"Gotta go. Stop worrying. I'll call you." Then, in a lighter tone: "And buddy, you owe me lunch when I find out you've sent me on a wild goose chase."

* * *

Not content to go home and wait to hear from Paul, and concerned for her sister's safety, Lea debated what to do. She turned to Gracie. The collie's head was hanging out the window, ears flapping in the wind, nose pointed straight toward the freeway.

"I agree, Gracie. We can at least drive in the direction of the campsite. If Maddy calls, we'll be that much closer to help."

Little did she know in her efforts to help her sister, Lea was placing herself in the area of no cell reception where she would fail to receive the call from Maddy that Roberto so urgently wanted her to get.

Chapter Eleven

They had been driving less than fifteen minutes but it felt like hours to Maddy. Bumping around in the back of the truck, she was exposed to trees along the side of the road. Oak and birch pollen was triggering every allergy she had, causing an itchy throat and making her eyes water.

Tossing from side to side in a last attempt to roll from under the dusty blanket, she sensed the truck slowing. She stopped moving, listening intently. She heard a horse whinny and a man's voice. The voice sounded vaguely familiar.

"How ya doin'?" the voice inquired casually of the driver of the truck.

Roberto responded in a neighborly manner: "Good, yourself?"

"Hate to tell you this but there's a tree down across the road just ahead. I passed it on horseback but you'll never make it around the tree with this truck. You got the riverbed on one side and a steep hill on the other."

"I need to get over the mountain to the interstate."

"You can turn around and go back to the coast highway. It hooks up with the interstate about fifty miles north."

"It takes twice as long going the coast route instead of the interstate. I don't have the time. I'm in kind of a hurry."

"Maybe you and I can move the tree off the road. If we can't do it ourselves, we'll put a rope around it. I can tie one end of the rope to my saddle horn and my horse will be able to pull the tree far enough off the road so you can get your truck through."

"Good idea. Let's try it."

Roberto starting climbing out of the truck. "Thanks, mister, I appreciate . . ."

Before he could finish the sentence, a loop of rope circled his upper body pinning his arms. He was pulled off his feet to the ground.

In the moment Roberto struggled to figure out what had happened, the stranger was on top of him, trussing him like a chicken with his arms and legs against his body.

"What in damnation are you doing?" Roberto screamed, anger spewing from every pore.

"I think you got hold of someone I know. I doubt if she's anxious to be spending any more time with you."

With that, Roberto's assailant walked to the back of the truck and pulled the blanket off the rolling, moaning lump.

"You got yourself in quite a pickle there, young lady." Amusement showed on his face as he began pulling the duct tape from across Maddy's mouth.

"Ouch, take it easy," she wailed. "You don't have to remove a layer of skin along with the tape."

"Your display of gratitude is underwhelming, to say the least," he laughed. Opening a pocket knife, he cut the tape away from her hands and feet. She refused his arm for support as she climbed from the truck.

"I'm fine, thank you very much," she announced haughtily, trying to regain her composure.

But in the first few steps, she found herself feeling woozy. She fell back into muscular arms that circled around to support her. Turning, she looked into the smiling brown eyes of her rescuer. The rancher from Maria's Donut Shop.

He stood a good four inches taller than Maddy. His hair was mostly covered by the black Stetson tipped back on his head. His smile displayed a dimple in his chin and the whitest teeth Maddy had ever seen.

Maddy feigned weakness. Swooning slightly, she allowed herself to fall against his chest. "Whoa, little lady. This has been an ordeal. Let's get you off your feet where you can catch your breath and clear your head."

He has taken my breath away, Maddy admitted to herself.

Leading her to the front of the truck, he opened the door and helped her inside.

"How'd you find us?" she asked, still shaken by the turn of events.

"I was doing my weekly ride along the back road beside the river. Homeless people hole up there during the dry season. Addicts get hold of drugs and go there to get high. And teenagers hang out there to," he looked over the top of his sunglasses, the corners of his mouth curling, "well, you know. I ride by to make sure they haven't left food that will attract animals living in the hills. I don't want coyotes coming this close to my property. It's easier if I get rid of the food."

"I still don't understand how you ended up in front of Roberto's truck."

"When I got close to the big sycamore, I saw a car I recognized pulled off on the side road leading to the picnic table."

"You knew it was my car from seeing us once at Maria's?"

Lowering his eyes and his voice, he looked into her eyes in a way that went right through her. "You were hard to forget even before I found you hog-tied and gagged in the back of a pickup truck belonging to one of the most notorious outlaws in the County."

Maddy's hair fell across her eyes, covering her flushed cheeks.

"When I found your car keys in the dust outside the car, I knew something was wrong. Being on horseback, I was able to ride down into the dry riverbed and follow it unobserved by Roberto to a point where I could get in front of him."

Kicking the boot of the trussed kidnapper, now dozing with his chin on his chest: "By the way, Roberto, there's no fallen tree. You would have had a clear getaway to the interstate. Now, let's give you a sample of how you treated this young woman and throw you in the back of your truck. There are some people anxious to get their hands on you."

Turning to Maddy: "If you can drive this truck back to get your car, I'll take it from there. I can tie my horse to the back bumper and give this hombre a ride to the police station."

"No problem," a revived Maddy assured him. She scrambled into the driver's seat as her rescuer wrestled Roberto to his feet and secured him in the back of the truck.

Watching him mount the beautiful golden chestnut, Maddy called: "It would be easier if I knew your name instead of calling you the man from Maria's or my knight in shining armor."

He rose in the stirrups, tapping a finger to the brim of his hat. "Scott. Scott Miller."

Before she could open her mouth to respond, he added: "You don't need to tell me your name. I got it from Maria the same day I saw you there, Maddy."

* * *

Approaching the turn-off, Scott and Maddy saw three parked vehicles and people, including Lea and Tom, milling around her car. Realizing she was driving the fugitive's black truck, Maddy started shouting and waving her hands out the window of the cab. A police officer at the scene had his weapon pulled before Lea recognized her sister and gestured wildly for Tom to call off his officer. Quickly appraising the situation, Tom ordered his officer to lower his firearm but they approached the truck cautiously from two sides.

Looking suspiciously at the man atop the chestnut mare, Tom opened the door of the truck for Maddy to step out.

"What in blazes is going on here, Maddy?" he demanded.

"Roberto was using me as a hostage to escape." She pointed in the direction of the cowboy in the black Stetson. "Until this gallant gentleman rescued me."

Before either of the men could respond, they heard the uniformed officer calling: "Hey, boss, come check out what's in the back of the truck."

"Aren't you a sight for sore eyes?" Tom exclaimed, seeing the object of their manhunt bound and gagged on the floor of the pickup. Walking around the truck, he reached to shake the cowboy's hand: "Tom Elliot. You must be the one I have to thank for this."

"Scott Miller," the stranger answered, dismounting his horse and looping the reins over the saddle horn.

Tom turned a stern but relieved gaze toward the slightly disheveled but beautiful woman beside him. "Now, Maddy, we're all waiting with bated breath to hear how you got yourself into this mess in the first place. But right now, I've got to take care of Mr. Ramirez."

Maddy gave the officer details while Tom transferred the prisoner from the truck to the patrol car.

Having secured the recalcitrant, Tom returned to Maddy placing his hands on her shoulders to get her full attention. "Need I tell you what you did coming out here was not only foolhardy but downright dangerous? I hate to think how badly this could have ended for you. Don't imagine for a minute Roberto would have let you go once we met his demands."

"Don't worry, Tom; I've learned my lesson," Maddy assured him.

Tom doubted this misadventure was enough to make Maddy change her ways. Daring by nature, she was obviously more exhilarated than frightened now that her ordeal was over. It made Tom realize her impulsiveness and sense of living in the moment were the very qualities that made her so appealing.

Lea headed for her car, calling over her shoulder: "Come on, Maddy. Follow me home. I have to let Paul know what's happened; then I want to hear every fascinating detail." She hesitated, turning back to Tom: "Unless, of course, you need her for something."

"No, go ahead." Tom turned to leave. "If I need more information from you, Maddy, I'll get hold of you tomorrow. For now, we're all just glad you're safe and unharmed."

Lea visualized the conversation Paul would undoubtedly want to have regarding the peril the sisters' amateur sleuthing had created for Maddy. Thinking a buffer might help, Lea called to Tom. "Meet later at the Crab Shack to hear the full version of Maddy's adventure and celebrate having all three brothers behind bars?"

"Yeah, that will probably work. Roberto's going to holler for his attorney right away like his brothers did so I won't be able to grill him tonight. I can turn the paperwork processing over to one of my minions. See you there at seven," he confirmed walking to the patrol car to confer with his officer.

"Would you care to join us, Scott?" Lea asked. "The least we can do is treat you to dinner after your heroic efforts on my sister's behalf."

"Thank you, ma'am, but my daughter's got a baseball game tonight I can't miss. They've got a chance to win their division and move on to the Little League playoffs."

At those words, Maddy's heart dropped from a level of great expectation to one of acute disappointment. So her handsome rescuer was married. How silly of her to have hoped that was not the case.

"Hopefully, we can do it another time. We're so grateful for what you did."

Giving her sister a hug, Lea's eyes teared. "I'm so thankful you're okay and nothing terrible happened to you. We'll see you at the Shack at seven."

Lea got in her car and drove off leaving Maddy alone with her rescuer.

"I hardly have the words to thank you. I realize the danger I was in and what might have happened if you hadn't come along to rescue me." She lowered her eyes demurely but before she could utter another word, she was wracked with an embarrassing onslaught of sneezing. "Sorry. It's the trees and dust. My allergies have kicked in."

Scott laughed. "Here, take this," he said, handing her the kerchief tied around his neck. "You wouldn't make much of a rancher."

As the police car drove past in front of them, Maddy shouted: "Hey, Roberto."

The prisoner looked out the window, a dark scowl on his face.

The woman's eyes blazed with anger. "Have a nice day," she said, extending her middle finger.

A grin spread across the cowboy's face. "You've got attitude, lady. I'll give you that."

He mounted his horse, waved over his shoulder, and rode off.

Chapter Twelve

Paul was the last to arrive at the Crab Shack. Lea knew she wouldn't be able to put off the anticipated lecture indefinitely but was glad of the opportunity to mellow him with a glass or two of his favorite wine.

Lea and Maddy recounted their meeting of the brothers at the donut shop and Maddy's later conversation with Maria which had led to her ensuing kidnapping by Roberto. Hearing about Maddy's rescue, Paul turned to Tom: "Scott Miller. Is that the Miller estate on the east side of town?"

"Yeah, do you know him?"

"I don't know Scott but I know his grandfather, Ralph Miller. One of my clients was interested in building single-family homes out there. He asked me to negotiate with Ralph to buy part of his property. The Miller Ranch is one of the biggest in several counties, more than twelve thousand acres. Have you seen the property?"

"Everyone in the County knows the Miller name but I never had cause on a jurisdictional level with them being outside city limits. On a personal level, I did have occasion to meet Miller and his daughter at one of those wine tasting events my ex used to talk me into attending. As far as seeing the Ranch, I've only driven past the fences surrounding the property."

"The terrain is remarkable: oak-covered hills, steep canyons, and the river valley. It's been in their family since the early 1900s. They started by raising grain and livestock. In recent years, they've branched into leasing parts of the land to the studios for movie and TV productions. They rent the Ranch House for special events like weddings, celebrity retreats, and political fundraisers."

"Your client was planning to build that far outside of town?"

"The concept was for each home to have an acre of land, big enough for people to grow their own food. We thought we had a chance because it was a big project for Miller and his daughter to handle."

"You're talking about Scott's mother? She helps run the Ranch?" Maddy asked.

"Yeah. Scott's father died of a heart attack not too many years ago. Right there on the Ranch. Keeled over one day when they were branding cattle. After her husband had his heart attack, she stepped up to help Ralph. I don't know if he could have kept everything going without her."

"That was a lot for her to take on."

"Oh, she's a strong woman alright," Paul acknowledged. "Besides her work at the Ranch, she's involved in community affairs. I've served on a couple of committees with her."

Maddy couldn't help being interested. "What's your impression of her?"

"Independent, strong willed, efficient at getting things done. She's also well liked and highly respected."

"What was their reaction when you asked about selling?" Paul asked.

"Ralph was in his seventies when we approached him. We figured he might be willing to sell out and retire like the other ranchers in the area. But the old man was stubborn. Wouldn't hear of having the land parceled off."

"What did his grandson think of the idea of selling?"

"Scott wasn't living here then. He and his grandfather had a falling out years ago. Ralph wanted his grandson to carry on the family tradition of ranching but his grandson had different ideas about what he wanted to do with his life. His mother encouraged him to follow his own dreams. The irony is Scott ended up with his own spread in Colorado."

"What brought him back here?"

"A couple of things from what his grandfather gave us as his reason for not selling. Ralph was still hoping his grandson would come back to work the Ranch with him for a few years before the old man lost his health. Then, tragedy struck and sealed the deal for Scott to return."

"What happened?" Maddy gasped.

"Scott's wife was killed in a tragic automobile accident seven years ago. Apparently, the couple was returning to their ranch from a weekend skiing trip when their car hit an icy patch in the road and skidded into a telephone pole. The five-year-old girl was uninjured and Scott walked away with a fractured collarbone, but his wife died on impact. After a year of mourning, Scott decided it would be best for his daughter to be surrounded by family who could help him raise her."

"How has it worked out for Scott being back here?"

"From all reports, he and his grandfather are really enjoying working together. His mother's been able to step back from the Ranch and get more involved in the community. And Scott's a devoted father to his young daughter."

Maddy's day had been a roller coaster of emotions and what she heard about Scott Miller sent her spirits soaring. She couldn't deny she would be attracted to the tall, handsome cowboy even if he hadn't saved her life. She was sure there had been chemistry between them during both of their recent encounters.

Her sister kicked her under the table while Paul was telling the story letting Maddy know Lea understood what her sister was feeling, a trait the sisters had shared since childhood.

Although Maddy would have liked to hear more about Scott Miller, Paul moved on.

"I assume from how you've described the way Neal and the Ramirez brothers worked their burglary operation that you won't recover any of the stolen goods. I'll have to inform the clients of mine who were victims."

"I'm sure they sold off the stuff after each burglary," Tom confirmed. "It was a pretty seamless operation. Or would have been once Neal had made enough money and disbanded the operation. If the van hadn't been abandoned at the Pier, we'd probably still be looking for the perps."

"Sounds like a pretty good motive for murder. If Neal was ready to quit and the brothers wanted to continue but couldn't do it without the information Neal was providing, it might have started a disagreement that ended in his murder."

"That was our initial view of what happened but when we couldn't place them close enough to the victim, we had to rethink what took place."

"What's your take on it now?"

"The coroner's report has come in. It confirmed a blow to the back of the head. Time of death was between nine and ten o'clock."

Lea's jaw dropped. "Whoa, shortly before the dogs found the body. If we'd arrived much sooner, I may have received a knock on the head myself."

Tom pointed a finger at her: "Or worse. You could have become a casualty of being in the wrong place at the wrong time."

Shivers ran the length of Lea's spine. "Were they able to identify the murder weapon?"

"From the marks left on the skull, the blow was caused by a blunt object, probably one of the rocks on the beach. I sent a couple of my guys to search for one with blood on it at the murder scene but no luck. The murderer probably threw it into the ocean where we'd have no chance of finding it. Even if it drifts back on shore, the blood will have washed off. The murderer destroyed any footprints by brushing strands of seaweed across them. Probably jumped on large rocks to make his or her way back to the Malecon."

"The blow was to the back of the head?"

"Yeah, so Neal wasn't facing his killer when it happened. That could mean one of two things. Either he was taken by surprise . . ."

"Or Neal was talking with his killer," Lea chimed in, "and his killer seized an opportune moment when Neal turned his back."

Paul leaned on his elbows, brow knitted in concentration. "If he was talking with the killer, he probably knew the killer. It could have been a stranger but it's an odd time of night for someone to be walking on the beach."

"Chances are Neal wouldn't have talked to the person, especially when he had his own business to take care of with the brothers," Lea reasoned.

Tom asked her: "What if a stranger approached you at night apparently seeking help?"

"As a woman, I'd exercise extreme caution. I'd ask from a distance if they were in need of medical assistance. If the answer was yes, I'd dial 911 for them. Otherwise, I would leave the scene immediately." Lea qualified her response. "Neal, having the typical male ego, probably wouldn't consider an approach from a stranger as a threat. But you haven't indicated signs of a struggle at the scene. You must be assuming Neal knew his assailant."

"Right again," Tom confirmed. "So the question that has to be asked is why the murder happened then and not another time. Why there and not somewhere else? Was it an argument gone wrong or the coming together of means, motive and opportunity?"

It was Maddy's turn: "If someone else knew about the meeting, it provided the perfect opportunity to do the crime and pin it on someone else at the same time."

"That suggests someone who knew about the burglary operation," Paul remarked.

"Someone who knew the vic intimately enough to have access to information they could use against him," Tom concluded.

Maddy clapped her hands. "You think he was being blackmailed by whoever found out."

Tom nodded. "Definitely an avenue we're exploring."

He paused as the waitress cleared their plates. "But I haven't told you the other interesting bit of information in the coroner's report."

Paul punched Tom lightly on the arm: "You've been holding out on us?"

"The blow to the head wasn't the cause of death. His neck was snapped."

Maddy gasped. "You mean Neal was strangled?"

"Yep."

Paul leaned back, crossing his arms across his chest. "Does that narrow the perpetrator to a man strong enough to strangle someone of Neal's height and weight?"

"It would except for the blow to the back of the head which rendered Neal unconscious or at least incapable of fighting back."

Tom's cell phone started buzzing indicating an incoming message. "Here's an update from the coroner now," he read. "Bruises on the victim's neck and chin show an outline of the strangler's hand including an object on one of the fingers, probably a ring. The Coroner also says from the position of the neck when the body was found, he should be able to tell me whether the strangler was right or left handed."

"Wow," Maddy exclaimed, "I didn't realize a strangler leaves that kind of evidence."

"Keep it in mind, Maddy." His eyes twinkled as he picked up his bill from the tray. "Even though you sometimes want to strangle me, you're bound to get caught if you do."

"Do you have to go so soon?" Lea asked.

"This evidence only helps me prove my case in court. Right now, I've got to get back to identifying the murderer."

"You don't think you have the killer with Roberto Ramirez in custody?"

115

"Roberto was talking at the station even before his attorney arrived. He's willing to take the rap for the burglaries but there's no way he's letting us pin the murder on him. He admits to having an arrangement with Neal for his brothers to steal merchandise and sell it over the border. The heist you busted, Lea, was supposed to be their last job. The purpose of the meet was to get their final payoff from Neal. They planned to stay in Mexico and not come back."

"So what was his explanation for what went down that night?" Paul asked.

"Says he drove his truck to the parking lot, the black one with the flames . . . your favorite new mode of transportation," Tom grinned, brushing against Maddy. "He waited for his brothers to show with the van.

When they came speeding into the lot and jumped out leaving the doors wide open, he knew something had gone wrong. The moment they told him they were being chased and he heard the crazy dog barking in the back of the van, he ran to where Henderson should have been waiting with the payoff. Neal was there alright. Lying dead in the sand.

He yelled at his brothers to leave the dog and abandon the van. They all jumped in his truck and took off. He drove them to the river to get their car. Roberto instructed them to drive to the border as fast as they could. He'd get the cash they needed and meet them in Mexico."

Paul was stunned. "Why didn't Roberto take the cash from Neal's dead body before he ran?"

"Oh, he tried. Frisked the corpse, being careful to cover his tracks, but there was no money. Either the murderer took it . . ."

"Or Neal never took cash to the meet," Paul suggested. "How ironic. He may have been planning to cheat the brothers out of the money they had coming, an ill-advised move but right in character for him. If that had happened, Roberto probably would have ended up killing him."

116

"That's how I see it," Tom nodded. "Roberto was ranting and raving all over the police station about what a crook Henderson was. He should have been thanking him. Neal getting himself killed undoubtedly saved Roberto from the gas chamber."

Chapter Thirteen

Talking with Lea on the phone the next morning, Maddy agreed Tom needed to have the information they had obtained from Liz about a visitor to Neal's office the night before his murder; however, she didn't agree with Lea's reasoning that she should be the one to tell him.

"If I tell Tom, it will either get back to Paul and I'll have some major explaining to do, or I'll have to continue to hide it from him. We intentionally omitted to bring it up at dinner last night but it could be important to Tom's investigation. You've got to do it, Maddy."

"Alright. But if Paul he finds out where Tom got the information, he'll be that much more convinced I'm the source of our sleuthing and a bad influence on you."

"We all know already you're a bad influence on me," Lea laughed, "but we all love you anyway. Got to run. Let me know how it goes."

Maddy knew she could stop by Tom's office but the setting of the police station for a conversation highlighted her involvement with the murder. She chose a more informal setting and created a plausible excuse for the meeting.

Tom answered on the first ring. "Tom Henderson. How may I be of service?"

"I'm impressed. Do you always answer your phone in such an official manner?"

Tom recognized the voice of the caller. "Hi, Maddy. Nope. That greeting is reserved for calls from the switchboard. As it happens, our receptionist is sick today so all the calls are coming through to me. But the offer is the same. How may I be of service?"

"It's been a long time since I've had that offer from a man," Maddy teased. "I could make lewd suggestions but I'm sure all your conversations are recorded."

Tom had the kind of laugh that made Maddy happy every time she heard it. "I'll make sure to edit this one before it's put in the archives."

"I don't want to take too much of your time so I'll get to the point of my call without further enticement. I want to talk you into displaying a couple of posters for the upcoming 'Food and Music under the Stars' fundraiser."

"You want to put posters on the bulletin boards here at the station?"

"Yes, please."

"I'm not sure this is the best place to find potential donors for your fundraiser. Most of the people passing through our station are stealing money, not giving it away."

"I'm thinking of the visitors who aren't dressed in orange. From sitting in the front room waiting to file a complaint last year, I remember reading every poster on your board. Two or three times, in fact."

"Are you implying you had a long wait before you were taken to see one of our officers?"

"Not complaining. But in planning where to display posters, I thought of every place in Buena Viaje where I've had to wait in a reception room. The police station is on the list, and you're my best contact there."

"Well . . ."

"To make my pitch more appealing, I'll make it in person and bring the posters but not to the station. Let me buy you a drink at the Hotel tonight; they have a buffet of free appetizers. Of course, there will be a lot of people there. Singles making a meal of the free goodies so they don't have to cook for themselves."

"I've been there once or twice myself. More for the drinks than for the food."

"So you know I'll be able to buy you two drinks for the price of one?"

"In my business, I have to be able to understand ulterior motives, Maddy. I've got you all figured out. But I'm a compliant benefactor so bring your posters. I'll make sure they get posted. See you there at seven."

"Better make it six thirty or all the food will be gone. Business people gather there after work. Unlike you, most people end their work day when the little hand is on six and the big hand is on twelve."

"I'll do my best. Fill a plate for me if you get there before I do."

"Will do. Thanks, Tom. I appreciate this."

"You're the one buying the drinks. Besides, it's no problem. You know I'm a pushover for you. You've just never come to grips with that. See you later."

Maddy was glad they weren't face to face so he could see the wave of heat she could feel rising from her neck to her cheeks. *Am I reading innuendos in Tom's last statement that weren't intended?*

* * *

Tom could have kicked himself. *What a dumb thing to say to Maddy. How had that slipped out? It's not how I think of her. She's a good friend, nothing more.*

It had been five years since Maddy's divorce and she had indicated no interest in getting entangled in another relationship.

Tom hadn't known Maddy when she was married; she and her husband lived miles away. But Tom's marriage fell apart shortly after Maddy's and when Maddy moved to Buena Viaje, Lea was instrumental in ensuring they had each other's shoulder to cry on.

Tom had been completely surprised by his wife's announcement she could no longer endure being married to someone in law enforcement. Only in retrospect did he recognize the signs that she hadn't been coping well with his long absences or the strain he was subjected to during intense investigations. As a homicide detective, he had to be able to control his emotions in order to handle encounters with brutal, sad, or senseless acts of violence. As a result, he had developed an emotional insulation that had driven his wife away.

Although he improved his attentiveness and emotional availability in subsequent relationships, he eventually resigned himself to casual friendships that called for less emotional involvement. His divorce and the broken relationships since had taught him one thing about women: it was easier having them as friends than having them as lovers.

Maddy was the best kind of friend. When she came into his life, she brought an essence important to him on several levels. She never failed to brighten his day and make him laugh. The carefree soul she was brought out his lighter playful side, a side he was infrequently able to display in his leadership role at the precinct. Most importantly, beside Lea and Paul, Maddy was the only one with whom he was willing to let down his guard.

Their relationship had evolved from a mutual pity party to discovering mutual likes and dislikes. Over time, their friendship blossomed into the kind few people are lucky enough to experience in a lifetime.

Am I willing to jeopardize that by acknowledging I have deeper feelings for Maddy? Besides, she's my best friend's sister-in-law. If I tried to have a relationship with Maddy and it went sideways the way the last one did, it could put a strain on my friendship with Lea and Paul. That's the last thing I want after all they've done for me.

After his divorce, Paul and Lea made sure he was included in their family outings. They also helped him through the period of binge drinking that followed the breakup of his marriage. It was one of the reasons they got together during the week for drinks and dinner. They understood his need to unwind from his stressful job. They made certain he did it with friends; not sitting alone in a bar, common in a profession where the divorce rate was fifty percent higher than for the general population.

Still, in spite of all the support they offered, they were a happily married couple. It had been Maddy who had brought him the most comfort during that time and kept him from going into a deep shell.

Maddy was the person he related to the most. Describing the end of her own marriage as a knockout blow she hadn't seen coming, she understood the shock as well as the anger of being taken by surprise. She empathized with his pain at having his world turned upside down. Other friends attempting to appear sympathetic seemed more relieved that they weren't in his shoes.

He and Maddy had recounted painful moments; first crying but eventually laughing, together. She gave him the freedom to express exactly what he was feeling without judgment. With her, there was no need to pretend he wasn't hurting or that he was coping well.

She even met him at the gym several times to spar, encouraging him as he released his anger and frustration on the punching bag. On nights when he couldn't sleep, she was a willing listener a phone call away.

Those meet-ups and phone calls had diminished in frequency once Tom began healing. It was Maddy who convinced him to wade into the dangerous waters of dating again. And it had been Maddy's counsel he sought after each failed attempt. Whenever she commiserated with him, she bolstered his ego making him feel he was a catch for any woman.

But has she ever considered me a catch herself?

* * *

Maddy arrived at the hotel in time to grab the last empty table. The bar stools were filled as well as the long couches in the middle of the lounge. The table she secured was barely big enough for two and pushed against the far wall, furthest from the bar and the buffet. It would be perfect to afford the privacy she needed to discuss murder, a conversation she didn't want overheard.

She put the posters across the chairs and advanced to the buffet table. As she had predicted, some hot food warmers were already empty but there was more than enough for them. She filled Tom's plate to the brim knowing it could well be his dinner and only meal of the day.

When she returned to the table, the waiter took her order of a vodka tonic and Tom's favorite beer. "Do you want the two-for-one on each of those?"

"Absolutely." If Tom had to return to work, he might not drink the second beer but it would be there if he wanted it.

Looking idly around to spot any familiar faces, her thoughts drifted to Tom's earlier remark.

She and Tom had always enjoyed bantering with each other, sometimes with sexual overtones, but the relationship they had was one of deep friendship. Tom was the brother she and Lea never had. She wouldn't trade having a sister, especially one like Lea, for anything in the world. But being athletic, she would have liked a sibling to share sports with. Tom provided that element for her, and more.

She liked to think their friendship was mutually rewarding. When questioning a woman as part of a murder investigation, Tom's read was impeccable. But in personal matters where emotions got involved, Tom got as rattled as every other man trying to understand a woman. It was always Maddy he turned to for advice and sympathy.

She had to admit that on more than one of those occasions, she had fantasized herself in a relationship with him.

"Hey, Maddy, how's my favorite girl?" She jumped, imagining he had entered her thoughts.

"Have you . . ." The waiter placed two frothy cold beers in front of him. "Guess that answers my question. Thanks for ordering. This is exactly what I need right now." He collapsed into the empty chair across from her.

Maddy regained her footing. "Besides my charming company?"

Tom grinned as he gulped down half a beer, licking the foam from his top lip. He pointed a finger at his raised mug: "All the more satisfying for drinking it in your company."

"Smooth as always, Tom," she smiled.

Watching him dig into the plate of food in front of him, she decided to broach her subject. Her fingers closed around her drink and she leaned closer.

"I'm not going to mince my words, Tom."

"Does that mean I was correct in thinking there was more to this meeting than posters? And you mincing your words," he grinned between mouthfuls, "would be a first."

Ignoring the sarcasm, she forged ahead. "Lea and I have information we feel you should have. I'm the one delivering it because Lea's worried Paul will be upset if he finds out we've been poking around in your investigation."

"He'd have good reason to be upset. And I hope you're not going to tell me that's what you've been doing."

Maddy knew Tom's words were simply a formality. He wasn't upset with her; he was only verbalizing what his friend would say if he were here. She rested her chin on her palm. "You know you can't resist getting information related to your case, especially from reliable sources like my sister and me."

Having emptied his plate, Tom leaned back to savor his second beer. "You realize I could have you arrested for obstruction of justice if you don't give me the information?"

124

"I'm here, aren't I?" She curled a strand of hair around her finger. Her mouth curved into a seductive smile.

"Okay, Super-sleuth. Let's hear what you've got."

"Neal had a visitor to his office late the night before his murder."

Tom's eyebrows furrowed as he sat straighter. "Interesting. Where did you get that information?"

"I can't reveal our source but. . ."

"Maddy." Tom's voice was firm in a way she couldn't ignore.

"Okay, okay. But real detectives never reveal the source of their information."

"You've got detectives confused with newspaper people. Now, unless you want to get in a world of trouble with me. . ."

"I got it. Our source is Neal's stepmother. She told us Neal and his father were in the middle of a somewhat troubling phone conversation when it happened. Neal was still at his office when he called. According to Liz, it was almost eleven o'clock."

"What was Neal calling about at that late hour?"

"Apparently, something to do with work. Harold was asking his son how he could help when Neal said someone was coming into his office. He told his father to disregard the call; he wouldn't need help after all."

"Did Harold follow up with Neal the next day?"

"He tried but Neal didn't return his calls until around dinnertime. Told his father not to worry. Everything was fine and he was on his way out for the night. It's the last they heard of Neal until they were told he'd been murdered."

"Did Harold have any idea who interrupted their conversation?"

"No. Harold knew so little of Neal's business; he wouldn't have known what meeting Neal had. Considering the time of night it occurred, it may have been a personal matter, but Liz wasn't aware of anyone Neal had become involved with since breaking off his engagement."

"How did you and Lea happen to be talking with Liz anyway?" The look he gave her would wither any suspect in his interrogation room at the precinct.

"She happened to come into the furniture store to see a new shipment of dining room pieces. . ."

"Happened to come in?"

". . . after I called her."

"Why didn't you tell me about this sooner?" The barely visible crow's feet around Tom's eyes became more pronounced, a sure sign he was not pleased.

"In case you forget, I was a little tied up, literally."

Images of Maddy trussed with duct tape and thrown in the back of the pickup truck came to mind. "By the way, have you heard any more from the rancher who saved your hide?"

"Nope." Maddy flirted to get back in his good graces. "Any particular reason for asking?"

"Just trying to keep you from getting hurt."

"Am I missing something here? That rancher, whose name you very well know is Scott, kept me from being hurt."

"And as you very well know, Maddy, there are different ways of getting hurt."

"Since when have you become my guardian angel?" she asked, giving him a lopsided grin.

"There could never be enough hours in my day to keep you out of harm's way, physically or emotionally," he winked, lightening the moment. "I'm only suggesting you haven't dated seriously since your divorce. I saw the way you looked at the cowboy. . . Scott. Like a damsel in distress being rescued by a white knight. Remember, you were both in a highly charged emotional situation."

He leaned forward. "Real life isn't like a fairy tale, Maddy. Relationships are difficult. I'm not sure a man who experienced

126

the heartbreak he went through with his wife's death is the right person for you to get involved with."

"I think you're reading too much into it."

"I doubt it. What makes me so good at my job is that I'm always observant. I pay attention to the smallest details. It's what enables me to draw conclusions others miss. I don't mind telling you, most of the time, those conclusions are correct. I noticed his eyes and his body language when he was around you. He's interested, Maddy."

He experienced an odd sense of disappointment when he saw her eyes light up hearing about Scott's reaction to her.

"You know I haven't had any interest in dating since that scuzzball Eric cheated on me and ended my visions of a once and forever relationship."

"It's been five years. Maybe it's time for you to try to find that kind of relationship again if that's what you're looking for. I'm just not sure this is the guy who can give it to you."

"Who else would you suggest?"

Tom's stomach plunged. His pulse raced. He looked deep into her eyes. "I don't know anyone I think is good enough for you."

Maddy tossed her long hair, feigning nonchalance. "What a flattering response, Tom, but it's a cop out. I guess we'll just have to see where things lead."

Her voice was cold as she stood and handed him the posters. "Thanks again for your help."

"Thanks for the drinks and your tip about Neal's visitor. Will you keep me informed if you and your sister find out anything else?"

"No problem, Detective." Maddy walked out, her fiery beauty drawing the attention of every man in the room.

Tom finished his beer, deep in deliberation. *Am I adding fuel to Maddy's fire by allowing her to become further involved in the murder case? Or is it a personal fire I just added fuel to?*

Chapter Fourteen

Lea was scanning the wall directory in the foyer of the City Hall building.

"What are you doing here? Official business or slumming?" a familiar voice asked.

She spun around. "Hey, Tom. Good morning."

She placed a hand on his arm in greeting. "The City is undertaking a public relations campaign to increase tourism. As an important historical landmark, City Hall itself will be portrayed as one of the major tourist attractions. I'm one of three people asked to submit a bid on the project which will include creating brochures and other promotional material."

"Good for you. That should be an interesting assignment."

"Yes, I really hope I'm awarded the contract. I've got a lot of good ideas. I'm anxious to get started."

It was her turn to question Tom: "I know you're not slumming but surely you're not here about the murder?"

"Not specifically, but there may be a connection." Tom took Lea's elbow, steering her out of the way of people trying to see the directory. "Neal was always able to tell his ring of burglars the best construction sites to hit. I'm thinking he may have had inside knowledge about where to send them."

"Who at City Hall would have that kind of information?"

"Anyone in the Planning Department. Applications for Building Permits include descriptions of the project, size, and timing of construction. With the right information, Neal could have determined what materials and equipment were on site. It would have taken the guesswork out of deciding which projects to hit to reap the biggest jackpots.

According to Ken Crosby, Don Carson had turned over all the work he did with City Hall to Neal. Neal would have frequent contact with people in the Planning Department. He may have persuaded someone there to pass on information he needed. For a price, I'm sure."

"I can't imagine anyone who works for the City doing such a thing."

"Most people have a price, Lea."

"You're getting too cynical, Tom. You sound like my sister. She's become a lot more skeptical and suspicious since she was cheated on.

Which reminds me . . . when I talked to her this morning, I suggested the four of us have drinks tonight at the Shack. She said she'd be busy. When I asked her plans, she admitted she didn't have any at the moment but insisted she'd be busy anyway. Sounds like she doesn't want to see you. You two have a difference of opinion, again?"

It wasn't unusual for Maddy and Tom, both strong-willed and opinionated, to experience frequent issues of contention. It sometimes presented a fractious dynamic to the relationship, similar to the way brothers and sisters spar.

"I met her for drinks last night so she could give me the news about Neal's late night office visitor. Thanks for that, by the way."

He noticed the look of concern in Lea's expression. "Don't worry; I won't divulge the source of my information to Paul."

"Thanks, Tom. You know how overly protective Paul can be," she said, smiling weakly.

"Have you ever considered that with you and your sister, there's reason for concern?"

"If that's the kind of thing you said to Maddy last night, I can see why she doesn't want to see you," Lea laughed, moving toward the elevator. "Gotta run. Talk to you later."

* * *

Lea's appointment was with Councilwoman Margaret Patton. As a Board member of the Buena Viaje Visitors and Convention Bureau, she was the point person representing the City whom Lea would be dealing with if she won the bid.

Lea made it a practice to familiarize herself with potential clients as part of the process of preparing a bid. To beat her competition, she felt she not only had to have the best product at the most reasonable price but she needed to present her proposal in a way that best resonated with the person receiving the bid. Even before entering the Councilwoman's office, Lea's research gave her the advantage of feeling like she knew this woman.

Mrs. Patton had grown up in Chicago where her father worked for the Federal government. Her parents divorced when she was five years old and her father moved to Washington, D. C. Her mother continued to work as a secretary in the government office where her parents had met. Even though her father paid support, they struggled financially and never had the financial freedom Margaret longed for. She envied her friends from wealthy families who were given cars in high school and bought all the beautiful clothes they wanted.

Margaret hated the cold winters and the hot summers of the Midwest. The day after her high school graduation she moved to California to live with an aunt in Los Angeles. She paid her own way through the local junior college and the state university by working for a catering company. She went from being on the wait staff to the position of Catering Manager through determination and hard work.

It was at an event her employer catered for a movie producer where she met her husband, a prominent actor more than twice her age. They married and had two children. When he retired from films, they built a large home in the hills outside Buena Viaje. She had been elected to the City Council three years ago and was known for her involvement in community events.

From her reputation, Lea anticipated a woman who was intelligent, independent, and assertive. Good with the public on one hand, she was also considered to be strong-willed, resolute, and determined. Detractors described her as ruthless and calculating. They held the view there were no wasted actions on the part of Mrs. Patton. Everything she did was done for a reason and to her benefit.

Perhaps her ambition comes from her history of not having all she wanted in her younger years. From outward appearances, she has it all now but people who overcome deprivation in childhood often harbor a subconscious fear of returning to the same condition.

* * *

"I appreciate your giving me the opportunity to bid on this project, Mrs. Patton."

"Call me Margaret, please," the woman responded cordially. She sat erect behind an enormous mahogany desk that seemed excessive for a woman of her diminutive stature.

Especially since there are no files, not even a single sheet of paper on the desk. Only a laptop computer. Either she's compulsively neat or this is a room where she holds meetings but does little work.

Impeccably dressed, makeup expertly applied, hair styled in the latest fashion and nails manicured, the woman across from her made Lea feel uncomfortably lacking in the elegance department.

"You do understand at least two other individuals or firms are bidding on the project," she said, her fingers drumming lightly but continuously on the top of the desk.

131

Nodding, Lea asked for clarification on one point before proceeding. "I know the last event in which the City was represented was the Protect Our Marine Life charity event at the Fairgrounds. I'm familiar with the firm who prepared the presentation for you. From my understanding, the slide show they presented on behalf of the City was well received. May I ask why you aren't using them again?"

"It's true the press gave favorable reviews of the City's presentation. Everyone at my table at the event made favorable comments. Of course, I don't know how grand an endorsement that was," she added, shrugging her shoulders. "The Mayor and the Planning Director were into their third cocktail by the time the City's slide show was presented."

Margaret threw the next comment off as an aside but Lea's ears perked up. "Neal and I were the only ones who paid much attention."

"Neal Henderson?"

"Yes, Neal was there representing Don Carson's company. I'm sure you're familiar with the County's largest developer?" she asked in a manner Lea felt was slightly condescending.

"I didn't realize City officials and developers socialize."

"The Mayor always sits at the front table. Charles White, the Planning Director, was there as the Mayor's guest. I wasn't there as a City Council member although the press reported it that way. I was seated there because of the size of the donation my husband and I made to the charity. Neal. . . Mr. Henderson . . . was at the table on behalf of Don Carson who has always made a sizable contribution."

Lea's intuition was on high alert to discover more about Margaret Patton's relationship with Neal Henderson. She hoped her next question wouldn't sound too obvious. "How generous of you and Mr. Patton. What did your husband think of the presentation?"

"Oh, Art wasn't there. He hates fundraisers. It doesn't stop us from contributing to almost every one of them. The only one he actually attends is the annual event to raise money for the local theatre. Other than that, he writes the check and I make a personal appearance. I've had more of those dinners than I care to remember."

Lea attempted again to get Margaret to talk about Neal. "Speaking of Mr. Henderson, what a tragic . . ." but was cut off as Margaret abruptly changed the topic of conversation.

"Yes, it was. But we've drifted off topic."

The Councilwoman clenched her hands in front of her and leaned forwarded. "In answer to your question, yes, we were pleased with the work done for us on that project. Nevertheless, we're required to receive bids for every project paid for with City funds. Let me make it clear. We're not required to award the contract to the lowest bid we receive but we do have a budget to comply with. I outlined the terms including the maximum amount of funding available for this project in the letter I sent requesting bids."

"Of course." Lea could sense pursuing further questioning was ill-advised. Besides, she was not given the opportunity.

The Councilwoman rose to her feet, picking up the written proposal Lea had placed on her desk. "I don't mean to be rude but I have a lot of work to do. Your bid will be taken into consideration with the others and you will be notified of our decision. Thank you for coming in."

Lea was impressed with this woman's directness, an asset to anyone with ambition. Mrs. Patton had come a long way. From a job as a catering manager to loathing catered events. A long way, indeed.

* * *

Tom was still waiting to see the Planning Director when he saw Lea descending the wide marble staircase. Telling the woman at the front desk he would return momentarily, he moved to catch her before she left the building.

"How did your meeting go? Did you knock 'em dead?"

"It felt pretty good but you never know. Sometimes a person has decided before you ever give them your proposal. They're only going through the protocol, wasting my time. Hopefully, that's not the case here and I have a real shot."

"You'll get it. You're the best." Tom was one of Lea's biggest fans, not because she was married to his closest friend but because she was intelligent, highly qualified, and a hard worker.

"You're an easy mark for a vote, Tom. All it takes is one of my home-cooked meals. But I can tell you one thing," she said, becoming more serious. "It would take something a lot more enticing than a home-cooked meal to bribe the Councilwoman."

"Now who's talking bribery? Aren't you the one telling me I'm cynical thinking anyone at City Hall could be bribed?"

"I'm not suggesting the Councilwoman could be bribed. But she's one ambitious, motivated woman. I'd hate to be the one to stand in her way when she makes up her mind to get something."

Tom's eyes narrowed. He looked at Lea intently. "That's an interesting comment, especially coming from you. You're the last person to criticize anyone."

"I'm not criticizing; merely observing." She lowered her voice. "Would you like to hear another observation?"

"You bet." Tom leaned closer so they couldn't be overheard.

"Mrs. Patton had feelings for Neal Henderson."

"How do you know?" Tom asked sharply.

"I don't know for a fact. It's only woman's intuition. You don't have to listen. Paul hates when I use that instead of logic as the basis for my reasoning."

134

"I'm a big believer in women's intuition. It's helped solve some of my toughest cases. Almost as reliable as Gracie letting me know who the bad guys are."

He put an arm around her, giving her a hug. "I'm especially glad to hear your instincts in this case because they jive completely with my own."

Lea's eyes widened. "What makes you say that?"

"Remember the picture I showed you that I found in Neal's condo?"

"Yes."

"There was another picture hidden behind it."

"So?"

"A picture of none other than the deceased and Councilwoman Patton sharing a cocktail."

Lea waved a hand, dismissing his comment. "She knows Neal from a business perspective because he was Don Carson's right-hand man. There would have been occasions for them to have a drink together."

"In the hot tub on the balcony of his condo?"

* * *

Tom's visit to the Planning Department was as unproductive as he predicted it would be. The Director was not in and his attempt to obtain information from the staff was fruitless. City personnel tended to close ranks when it came to outsiders, especially those representing other official agencies. He knew without the authorization of a warrant, he was unlikely to find anyone willing to be forthcoming enough to confirm his suspicions.

But he had another weapon in his arsenal. He punched a number on his cell and left a message asking Paul to meet him at the gym for a workout.

He followed the wide circular staircase to the second floor. Entering Councilwoman Patton's office, he flipped open his badge case for the middle aged, gray haired woman sitting at the front desk. She introduced herself, adding his card to other cards in a bowl beside her computer. "Rosemary Hanson."

"I need to speak with the Councilwoman, please."

"I'm afraid you missed her. She left for a luncheon. Won't be back until late afternoon."

"This won't wait. Where is her luncheon?"

The woman hesitated. Tom could see her mental wheels churning, deciding what to do. Having a policeman show up at the luncheon was out of the question.

"Perhaps you can talk with her on her cell phone. She should still be en route. Let me see if I can reach her." She put the call on speakerphone so they both heard the curt answer.

"What is it, Rosemary?"

"Mrs. Patton, I have Detective Elliot here. He needs to speak with you. I've explained you're busy until late afternoon but he insists he sees you. Rather than have him go to the luncheon you're attending, I've taken the liberty to put him in touch with you by phone. I hope that's acceptable."

Does everyone walk on eggshells around this woman?

There was a pronounced silence. After several seconds, a clipped voice came through. No effort was made by the speaker to be cordial. "My secretary is correct, Detective. I won't be in my office until after four and I have appointments scheduled for the rest of the day."

Tom's response was immediate and forceful. "I have questions about the recent murder of Neal Henderson. Your schedule for the rest of the day is not my concern. We can do this at your office at four o'clock or you can come to the police station to be interviewed. The time isn't open for negotiation. The place is your choice."

Another lengthy pause. "My secretary will reschedule my appointments. I'll see you at four o'clock at my office, Detective." The line went dead.

The secretary switched off the speaker. Tom noticed the Councilwoman hadn't given her instructions directly to the secretary. It was assumed they had been heard and would be carried out.

"Is she always like that, Rosemary?" Tom's intentional use of her first name encouraged her confidence.

Looking up, she allowed a slight smile to flicker across her face. "This gray hair has been righteously earned, Detective."

"Have you only worked for her during her tenure at City Hall?"

"Oh, no. We go back much further. I've worked for her in one capacity or another for the last twenty years. Personal Assistant, Social Secretary, part-time Nanny to her children when they were young. I first worked for Mr. Patton when he was making movies. When he semi-retired and moved here, he insisted I come along. He made the down payment for me to buy a house. It was a real godsend at the time. I was a single mother raising two kids on my own."

"He sounds like a generous person."

"It's the way he's been ever since I've known him. Generous in many ways. He helped a number of young actors get started in their careers.

He's modest, too. Never took credit for all the honors and accolades he won. Insisted his fine acting was the result of the directors, his fellow actors, and the technical crews."

"Is he involved much in the community?"

"Well, he wouldn't tell you but I will. He's the major benefactor to the local theatre group. His donations are what keep it going.

But once he got away from the environment of the studios and all the public relations activities required of him as a big star, he began to enjoy his solitude more and more. He withdrew from community activities and let his wife take over. He's content now growing his roses and showing his dogs. I believe he's more proud of the first in show ribbons his dogs have won than of all the gold statues the picture industry awarded him."

"Is his wife as generous?"

Her answer was blunt: "Nope. He's the one who writes all the checks for charities. She's much tighter with the purse strings except when it comes to her wardrobe or the dinner parties she likes to host."

"You don't seem to be a huge admirer. How did you come to work for her?"

"Simple supply and demand, you might say. He needed me less and less. She needed someone more and more. He was grateful to have someone he trusted who was . . ." She stopped short, putting her hand to her lips.

"Willing to put up with her?" Tom finished.

"Don't think I'm talking out of school. They both know how I feel. I'm happy to do it to repay all the kindness Mr. Patton has shown me through the years."

"I appreciate your candor. It helps me get a better picture of who I'm dealing with. One last question. How well did the Councilwoman know Neal Henderson?"

"That I can't help you with. She kept her personal affairs private."

Tom's eyebrow rose. *Was her choice of words intentional?*

"You don't have to mince words with me, Detective. You want to know if the Councilwoman had an affair with the deceased. If Mrs. Patton had any indiscretions, she would be especially careful about letting me be privy to them knowing how close I am to Mr. Patton. As far as I know, Neal Henderson came to her office once or twice but only on the pretext of business."

"What business?"

"As I recall, he was here to discuss some business with the Planning Department, asking her advice on how best to handle something. An arrogant sort of fellow, but he behaved with propriety."

Tom thanked her and jogged down the sweeping stairs of the city offices. The time spent with Rosemary Hanson had more than compensated for his lack of results at the Planning Department. He wished all his interviews were as productive.

Still, he had to ask himself: *Was Rosemary's disapproving caricature of Mrs. Patton prejudiced by her own feelings for her benefactor?*

Driving out of the parking lot, Tom enjoyed a sense of making progress. Regardless of the accuracy of her secretary's portrayal, he was even more eager for his upcoming interview with the Councilwoman.

Chapter Fifteen

"What do you want, Paul?" Lea answered snappily.

"You to be happier to hear from me for starters."

"Sorry. I already got an email from Councilwoman Patton saying someone else has won the bid." She sounded more than disappointed; she sounded angry.

"Sorry to hear that, babe."

"I'm going to call to make an appointment to see her. I worked hard on this proposal. It's one of the best I've ever done. I was more certain I would win this one than any other I've submitted. I'd like to know why I didn't get it."

"You've lost bids before and you usually aren't given a reason. Why is this different?"

"For one thing, because the rejection came so quickly. My gut is telling me the woman rejected my bid to keep me from asking more questions about Neal Henderson. It's not fair."

It was Paul's turn to be angry. "You asked the Councilwoman about Neal Henderson? What are you talking about, Lea?" he demanded.

Lea was put on the defensive. "She mentioned him in the course of the conversation. All I did was ask a few questions about their relationship."

"Their relationship? What relationship?" Paul asked incredulously.

Lea refused to explain herself to her doubting husband by admitting her conclusion was based on intuition.

"Something she said made me think she knew Neal on a level other than business."

"Made you think?" His voice left little doubt; Paul was irate. "Don't you mean your so-called woman's instinct kicked in

140

causing you to insult the Councilwoman by making an untoward implication?"

"My reason for asking questions wasn't so obvious," she countered, trying to placate him.

"It was apparently obvious enough she awarded the bid to someone else. Undoubtedly to keep you from pestering her further by taking away the opportunity you might have had to work with her."

Lea barely heard his words as her anger slowly turned to excitement. "But don't you see, Paul? If that's why she denied me the bid, and I don't believe there was any other valid reason, it proves she has something to hide. Why else would it bother her to answer any questions I had about Neal?"

"I think this entire episode proves that your overly inquisitive nature . . ."

"Go ahead and say it. Don't you mean my amateur sleuthing as you like to call it?" she suggested, trying to lighten the tone the conversation had taken.

"I could use a better description, like butting into other people's business. Whatever you choose to call it, it's become a detriment, first to Maddy's safety, now to your profession." Lea could hear Paul taking deep breaths, trying to calm himself.

"Have you ever considered it might be my true calling rather than being a business writer?" she giggled, trying to restore his good mood.

"Not even for a moment."

"Nevertheless, I'm going to see the Councilwoman to find out why I lost the bid," she announced stubbornly.

"Fine." Lea could hear the exasperation in his voice. "I'm only wasting my breath trying to talk you out of it. I'll see you tonight. But please, may I ask one thing?"

"Of course, sweetheart, anything," she purred.

"When you see her. . ."

"Did you say when?"

"Yes, when, because I know regardless of what I say, you're determined to charge ahead." The anger in his voice was replaced with concern. "I'm only asking you to dial it down a notch and stay out of trouble."

"No problem. Tell you all about it when you get home tonight."

Grabbing her purse and keys, she called for Gracie. "Maybe you better come with me, girl, to help me keep my promise to Paul."

* * *

Certain the Councilwoman wouldn't agree to a meeting if she called ahead, Lea decided to go to City Hall on the off chance an opportunity to see Mrs. Patton would present itself. She parked in the lot reserved for visitors, opened the tailgate, and walked the border collie to a grassy area.

Chuckling, she gave the dog instructions: "You do your business, Gracie; then I'll go inside and do my business."

Lea turned her gaze toward the front of the building as the dog squatted. Hurrying down the front steps toward a black limousine parked in the loading zone was none other than the object of Lea's visit.

Yanking at Gracie's leash, Lea ran toward the front steps. "Councilwoman . . ."

The dog caught up and was pulling Lea across the slope leading to the sidewalk where the limo was parked. "Mrs. Patton, could I have a minute, please?"

The woman turned, surprised at hearing her name called, and more surprised at the sight of the woman running toward her behind a small mass of gold and white flying fur. "Lea, is that you? What in the world . . ."

Lea apologized, breathlessly: "I'm sorry. I was coming to make an appointment to see you." Ignoring the woman's stern

142

look, she plunged ahead: "To find out why I wasn't awarded the bid."

Realizing how unreasonable her request may have sounded, she added: "I understand, of course, you obviously found someone more qualified or at a better price but I want to make sure it wasn't because of my presentation."

Lea was suddenly aware of how foolish she must appear. Her hair was flying in all directions and she was perspiring. "What I mean to say is, if I know the reason I wasn't chosen, it would help me improve presentations to future prospective clients."

She tried to smooth her hair with one hand while holding Gracie's leash with the other.

The Councilwoman raised herself to her full height, glaring at Lea: "All you are entitled to know is the bid was awarded to someone else. I'm not in the habit of discussing my decisions with anyone. I have nothing else to say on the matter except I have no time for this. I'm late for an appointment of my own."

Turning abruptly, she gave instructions to the uniformed man holding open the door of the limousine: "Let's go, Max. I'm in a hurry."

Without thinking, Lea moved toward the car in a last attempt to speak further but the Councilwoman had slipped into the back seat. The driver shut the door and turned quickly. Grasping one beefy arm with the other and extending both arms in front of his body, he blocked Lea. "Sorry, ma'am," he spoke brusquely. "The Councilwoman can't talk with you."

The low rumbling emanating from the dog drew the attention of both Lea and the driver.

"Gracie, hush," Lea commanded, surprised and embarrassed. "Don't worry," she assured the man as she yanked the leash. "The dog's friendly. Sorry for the interruption."

Lea leaned over to offer the Councilwoman a placating smile but the tinted windows prevented her from seeing in. She and Gracie stepped away from the vehicle as the driver rounded the car and took his place in the driver's seat. In seconds, the vehicle pulled away from the curb and sped out of sight.

Lea saw Gracie was in guard mode, fur bristling, ears pointed, and tail rigid.

"Wow, easy, girl." She patted the dog's head. "Who got your dander up? The Councilwoman or her driver?"

Back at the car, Lea got Gracie settled in giving her a hug to relieve her tension. "From your reaction, I'd say her driver is more of a bodyguard than a chauffeur."

* * *

Maddy had time to kill before meeting Lea for lunch.

Her sister had called earlier, breathless with excitement. "Wait until you hear about the interesting encounter I had this morning."

"I can hardly hear you, Lea. Are those dogs barking?"

"Yeah. I'm at the pet groomer with both dogs. Can't talk now. What time do you get off for lunch?"

"I'm meeting a client at noon to pick out carpet samples. I'll be done by 1:00."

"The Diner?"

"Sounds good. See you there."

* * *

Maddy's appointment at the carpet factory had gone well and she'd sent her client packing with an armful of samples. "I think I've earned a reward. What will it be? Truffles or bonbons?" she asked herself, staring into the window of the chocolate shop.

"That stuff isn't good for you."

The unexpected voice over her shoulder made her jump. She whirled around and found herself staring up at a handsome familiar face. This close, she could see flecks of silver in his eyes. She took a quick step backward.

Recovering quickly, she flashed her most dazzling smile as the man tipped his hat. "So now you're looking after my health as well as my safety?"

Scott Miller's eyes creased in a smile. "Why don't you let me take you to lunch at the vegetarian place where you can have something healthy to eat?"

"Thanks for your concern regarding the state of my health, but I'm meeting my sister for lunch." Hoping it was disappointment she saw reflected in his face, she added quickly: "I suppose I have time for a carrot drink."

She moved into step beside him: "Don't look so surprised. I actually take care of my body when I'm not putting it in harm's way as I've been accused of doing lately."

He gave her a once over. "Oh, I'd say you take great care of your body."

Blushing, she stuck her nose in the air. "I'm surprised you know about the Healthy Planet. I would have figured you for a meat and potatoes man."

He gave a half smile, the kind of smile that made her want to see more of it. "Because I'm a rancher? That's a cliché. Raising cattle doesn't mean meat is all we eat."

He touched her elbow gently when the light changed, guiding her across the street. When they entered the restaurant, it was filling quickly, a line forming at the order counter.

"Get us a booth. I'll order your carrot juice."

He returned in moments, setting a glass with orange liquid in front of her. Sliding into the booth across from her, he removed his black Stetson running a hand through his thick, curly hair. She noticed the cowlick at his hairline.

"That stuff isn't good for you," she mimicked, watching him lift a mug to his mouth.

"If you must know, it's not coffee; it's green tea."

He turned the mug slowly as he spoke. All of his movements seemed relaxed and fluid.

"So, Ms. Maddy. I'm learning all sorts of things about you." He leaned back, scrutinizing her. "You like chocolate but force yourself to drink carrot juice because it's good for you."

"How do you know I'm forcing myself to drink carrot juice?"

"From the way your nose crinkles every time you put the glass to your lips."

Her cheeks turned pink a second time as she rested her chin in her palm.

Amusement glistened in his eyes as he continued. "You've got dust allergies so you probably work out at a spa in town instead of hiking in the country."

Is he laughing at me?

He stared at her a long moment. "I bet you're not a morning person either."

A vision of what the man sitting across from her might look like in the morning flashed in her head. She looked into the dark, penetrating eyes of Scott Miller and knew he had no trouble reading her thoughts.

"How would you know?" she demanded.

He gave a simple explanation. "Because you work in retail, not in an office. It means you go to work later in the morning and sometimes work at night."

"I suppose you're up and about at the crack of dawn?" she replied testily, trying to turn the focus of the conversation away from her.

"I'm usually out on the range with my foreman by six o'clock checking to see if we had any problems during the night."

A smile returned to her lips. "You mean people actually carry on conversations at such a ghastly hour?"

Scott laughed. "Many people do, yes."

"What kind of problems would you have during the night?" she asked with interest.

146

"Coyotes coming down from the hills to make a meal of one of the sheep or young calves."

She grimaced: "Why would anyone in their right mind leave a perfectly comfortable bed in the middle of the night to view a grim sight like that?"

Amusement shone in his eyes. "Because it's part of a rancher's job."

She gave a lopsided grin: "Maybe ranchers don't have the right incentive to stay in bed."

He stroked his chin. "I can see you're a handful, but sort of a delightful one."

"What else do you think you know about me, or should I ask what else did Maria tell you?"

"She told me you're not married or we wouldn't be sitting here having this conversation. Don't worry, I didn't ask for details."

"I don't mind talking about my divorce." She twisted the ring on her middle finger. "I met Eric when I was living the fun life of a single person in the big city. Unfortunately, he was married when we met but he didn't let that stop him from pursuing me and frankly, I wasn't above having an affair with a married man. I never expected anything to come of it."

"How did you go from having an affair to being married?"

"His wife found out about us and left him, taking their two children. Eric's the type man who has to be married; he can't wake up in the morning without a woman beside him. So he talked me into it."

"Sounds like you weren't ready to be married."

"Eric and I were opposites in that regard. I enjoyed the single life. I had a great job at the Design Center so I was financially independent. I could travel whenever I wanted. I had a group of friends I socialized with for entertainment: rock climbing, mountain biking, Lakers games, restaurant and bar hopping."

"What about starting a family?"

"My sister inherited the maternal genes. She married when she was twenty and had their son when she was twenty-two. Eric's ex moved to San Francisco but he had visitation every other week and alternating holidays. Being a stepmother was more than enough parenting for me. I liked his kids but their mom was bitter over his affair. She made it difficult for them to accept me without feeling disloyal to her."

"That's rough. I've seen too many children put in situations where they're made to feel they have to choose between Mom and Dad."

He's listening and putting himself in my shoes. It's one of the things I like about him. "The kids and I found a way to make our relationship work. They weren't the reason the marriage fell apart."

She curled a strand of hair in her fingers; then let it fall place in place. "When I made up my mind to marry Eric, I convinced myself he wouldn't cheat on me the same way he cheated on his ex. When it happened, I wasn't terribly surprised but it didn't make it any less painful."

"How long were you married?"

"Eight years. The first six were good. I could have left sooner but I try not to play the 'could have, should have' game with myself."

"Why didn't you stay in the city? You enjoyed living there."

"It wasn't the same. All my single friends were married by then. The excitement of living in a big city had worn thin; too much traffic, pollution, overcrowding. Maddy and Paul had moved to Buena Viaje to be closer to his parents. During visits with them, I grew to love this quaint little town and the uncrowded beaches. It seemed to be the right place and the right time. Eric bought out my equity in the condominium we owned. I bought a cottage close to the ocean and have never looked back."

"I can relate to the right place and the right time. That's how I ended up here myself."

148

"I'd like to hear about that. It's your turn."

He was quick to change the subject. "Maybe next time. Aren't you supposed to be meeting your sister?"

She'd lost all track of time. "I better go."

"I'd still like to buy you lunch. Call your sister and ask her to join us."

Her smile faded. She turned her head to hide her disappointment. *If he's willing to have Lea join us, he's not interested in having me all to himself, the way I feel about him.*

"Sure," she answered nonchalantly, punching a number into her phone.

"Hey, Sis. Change of plans. Meet me at The Healthy Planet. Scott Miller is treating us to lunch," adding crustily, "if you're willing to put up with his cheekiness."

* * *

Once Lea joined them, the three of them stood in line and placed their orders from the wooden menu hanging on the wall. The women returned to the table placing their assigned number where the server could see it while Scott collected napkins, plastic utensils, and bottled water.

The table had two booths creating an awkward moment for Scott to choose which woman to sit beside. Without missing a beat, he dragged an empty chair across the floor, positioning it at the end of the table. He grabbed his hat from the booth and hooked it on the back of the chair. He and Maddy shifted around after bumping knees under the table.

"So what's the big news you wanted to tell me?" Maddy asked half-heartedly.

Lea hesitated, her eyes darting from Maddy to Scott and back to Maddy.

"Oh, it's alright," Maddy said petulantly. "You can talk in front of him. He's harmless."

149

Lea noted the dynamic between the two with interest but pitched into her story. She related her first meeting with the Councilwoman and their strange run-in that morning, including her dog's reaction.

"To be honest, when her chauffeur stepped in front of me to prevent my talking to her, it gave me the creeps," Lea shivered.

Maddy placed her hand over her sister's arm. "You poor thing. What a nasty scene."

"I don't know which of them provoked Gracie more, the Councilwoman or her chauffeur."

"As I told you before, Lea, your dog has good instincts," Scott cautioned. "Max is a tough guy; somebody you don't want to mess with. He's been a driver and a bodyguard for the Pattons for as long as I can remember."

"You know him?"

"Most people around here do. Maybe not the crowd you run with but there are several places in town where men run into him."

Maddy drew back in surprise. "Exactly what kind of places are you referring to?"

When he started to grin, she narrowed her eyes at him.

"I mean places like the gym, the shooting range, and the karate studio. He's a Black Belt and a crossFit expert."

His expression turned serious. He flicked his eyes from Maddy to Lea and back. "I repeat. He's a guy you don't want to mess with."

They finished their lunch and Scott headed for the door. Maddy felt deflated. It seemed obvious he had no interest in pursuing a relationship. She was putting on her sunglasses when she saw him turn and walk back to their table. Her heart pounded as he leaned over her: "I forgot to ask. Do you have a phone number you might be willing to share?"

Chapter Sixteen

Tom and Paul entered the patio area outside the gym after their workout. With few people using the equipment at that hour, they were able to put in a vigorous session. They were alone at the snack bar as they relaxed with an energy drink.

Paul stretched his arms over his head. "I'm assuming your asking to meet now instead of our regular noon workout was to avoid the crowd."

"Both from the standpoint of the workout and because of the conversation we're about to have which needs to be confidential."

"Why do I feel this is going to lead to your asking for a favor?"

Tom grinned, kneading his shoulder. "Because you know me so well."

"What's up?"

"I know you spend time at City Hall representing your clients in one capacity or another. What about the Planning Department?"

"My clients typically have someone on their staff designated to submit Plans and obtain Permits. But yes, on occasion, my clients ask me to take care of those issues."

"Do you have any connections there you might be able to get information from?"

"Depends on what kind of information you're after."

"Okay, let me lay it out for you and you can decide if you can help." Tom wiped his towel over his face and arms. "Neal Henderson's criminal activity may have gone deeper than we first thought."

"What do you mean?"

"There may have been a three-legged collusion for mutual gain between someone in the Planning Department, a member of the City Council, and Neal."

"Are you talking about a possible pay-to-play scenario?"

"Yep. Information has recently come into my possession which leads me to suspect Charles White, the Planning Director, received favorable treatment in the form of cash or other benefits from Neal in exchange for approving Permits for Don Carson's projects." Tom tipped his head back, draining the last of his protein drink. "As you know, money exchanged for services or the privilege to engage in certain activities has been uncovered in a lot of industries; certainly not unheard of between developers and Planning Departments."

"Sadly, you're right. I recall several cases, but it's hard to believe it's happening here."

"I'm not suggesting outright money bribery but there may have been more subtle exchanges of gifts or other benefits."

"Why do you think Charles White is involved?"

"There's only one person in a position to directly influence the approval of Building Permits: the Planning Director. Many of the Plan Approvals granted by the City Council are based solely on his recommendation."

"Wow, I'm stunned," Paul said, shaking his head. "What got you started on this?"

"As part of our murder investigation, we got a court order to access Neal's bank statements. There were several large withdrawals of cash in the two or three weeks preceding his death.

At about the same time, we received an anonymous tip that the Planning Director had accepted a twelve thousand dollar membership from the Golf Club during the time Neal was lobbying for approval of his Building Plans. If it's true, it qualifies as the Planning Director's illegal receipt of a gift from a developer in exchange for Permits. At a minimum, grounds enough to cost him his job."

"How much in cash incentives are you talking about?"

"The cash withdrawals were for fifteen thousand, eleven thousand, and nine thousand dollars. We haven't been able to track where the cash ended up. I'd love to be able to take a look at Mr. White's bank records but without any real proof, I have no grounds to secure a warrant. At any rate, he's probably hidden any large influxes of cash in a separate account to avoid detection."

"Do you know what specifically the payoffs were for?"

"Neal was managing two large projects for Carson Development prior to his death. Mr. White was responsible for assessing and making recommendations to the City Council on both of those Development Applications.

"What were the projects? I may be familiar with them."

"Victoria Square is one of them."

"Yes, I've heard about it. A mixed-use project proposed to be built on the hillside above the downtown area. Residential units, retail space, and a parking garage."

"That's the one. Plans indicate projected costs to be in the range of eighteen million dollars.

"The other is The Quarter, an apartment project in midtown with estimated costs of ten million."

"So you're talking considerable money at stake."

"Apparently considerable enough to convince the City Planner to risk losing his job by accepting bribes."

"You said you think it was a three-party scheme."

"I think Councilwoman Patton may have been the third party."

The shock showed on Paul's face. "What makes you say that?"

"I have reason to believe Mrs. Patton and Neal were involved in a personal relationship." Tom paused: "It may have started innocently enough as a mutual physical attraction, a fling. It fit right into his profile of being a Casanova. Once in the relationship, Neal realized what a perfect opportunity it afforded him."

"Could it have been Neal's plan all along to entice the Councilwoman into a relationship for the sole purpose of personal gain?"

"We'll probably never know if Neal pursued her solely from honest attraction or if he had ulterior motives from the outset."

Paul considered what Tom was suggesting. "But she wouldn't have been in a position to assure him Permit approval directly."

"That's correct, but I believe she was instrumental in bringing Neal and the Planning Director together so they could work out a mutually beneficial enrichment scheme."

"It was a pretty daring move on her part. She would have been in serious trouble if the Planning Director had reported she approached him."

"Probably not as risky as it might appear. The tip we received suggested even though Mr. White knew Mrs. Patton and Mr. Henderson had a friendship involving dinner dates, he never questioned them about the relationship or reported his suspicions to the rest of the Planning Department staff or the City Council. The fact he took no effective action to deal with Mrs. Patton's apparent conflict of interest sent a signal to the two of them that the Director was approachable regarding his own involvement in a possible pay-for-play scenario."

Paul leaned back, taking a deep breath: "Quite a scheme, if it's true."

"Between the three of them, they had the bases covered. If Plans were required to go before the City Council for approval, the Councilwoman was in the perfect position to ensure their success. Then, as different phases of the projects were completed and ready for Final Permits, Neal used his influence with the Planning Director to make sure those Permits were approved."

"Those are pretty serious accusations, Tom."

"And not ones I'm ready or even willing to make. There's no question if the Planning Director took compensation in exchange for favorable actions, both he and Neal Henderson committed a crime. At a minimum, it's reasonable to suspect both he and the Councilwoman were guilty of giving Neal Henderson information which shouldn't have been given."

"But those crimes are out of your area of expertise," Paul suggested, "and even if the District Attorney launches an investigation into Planning Department abuses, it could continue for years without results."

"Exactly right. That's why I'm not interested in the bribery side of the whole sordid mess except in one key aspect."

"Which is?"

"In my thinking, possible exposure of duplicity by either Mr. White or Mrs. Patton could be a motive for murder."

"What can I do to help?"

"My problem is I have no proof. Without it, I can't get anyone to open up about what was going on. The Planning staff understandably fear losing their jobs by blowing the whistle on their Director's wrongdoing. Until staffers are confidentially interviewed as part of a criminal investigation, the full extent of agency wrongdoing will remain undisclosed."

"What can you do in the meantime?"

"All I need now is sufficient presumptive evidence to put enough pressure on Charles White or Margaret Patton to break this thing open."

"What do you want me to do?"

"Keep your eyes and ears open for anything that might provide what I need."

"What specifically are you looking for?"

"Any signs of impropriety in the Department the staffers may have noticed."

"Why do you think they'd tell me?"

"Because of the anonymous tip we received. Someone has seen something they think is illegal, but they don't want to be a whistleblower."

"Any way to identify the caller?"

"Whoever placed the call was careful. We hoped tracking the call would lead us to an extension at City Hall but it traced to a burner phone. The call came in late, after office hours. It was a woman's voice. No identifying inflections or speech pattern."

"Doesn't narrow it down much, but I'll see what I can do. Anything else?"

"My gut is telling me Charles White was the late visitor to Neal's office the night before his murder. Maybe delivering Neal's Permits in exchange for a cash payoff. It would account for Neal being in a good mood the next day as his stepmother reported."

"I'll nose around and see what I find." Doubt crossed Paul's face. "I suppose I do appear less imposing than you."

Tom put on a tough guy face. "Oh yeah. I'm Mr. Intimidation. You're Mr. Nice Guy."

"That's what I hear from my wife all the time," Paul grinned. "It's why I get no respect at home."

"I get the same amount of respect from your wife's sister, believe me."

"You mean as in none."

"I mean as in none."

The two men laughed as they headed for the locker room.

* * *

Paul stood outside the Planning Department excited he'd been able to obtain information that should prove helpful to Tom's

156

investigation but unwilling to walk away without digging deeper into the Planning Director.

He understood Tom's reluctance to investigate further into possible corruption in the Planning Department; it wasn't the Detective's bailiwick and most likely had nothing to do with the murder. But regardless of his friend's position in the matter, Paul felt a need to determine for himself if there was any truth to the allegations. He felt an obligation on behalf of his clients, most of whom had dealings with the Planning Department. If there were improprieties in the issuance of Plan Approvals or Permits, his clients could be treated unfairly. On a personal level, even the intimation of duplicitous behavior affronted his sense of integrity in business.

Paul considered his strategy. *The Director doesn't know the police won't pursue allegations of misconduct. If I drop an intimidating hint, he may tip his hand.*

He returned to the counter and asked to see the Director on the premise of seeking approvals for a client's recent Plan submissions. Agreeing to a fifteen to twenty-minute wait, he was escorted into an inner office where a secretary worked at a small desk beside a door with the nameplate Charles White, Planning Director. He had met the man on one previous occasion when a client had introduced them. It was a brief exchange and Paul doubted the Director would remember him.

The secretary introduced herself as Marcia Thomas and quickly resumed her work. Paul sat on a metal chair next to a table with an assortment of outdated magazines. Leafing through one of them, he was able to observe her more closely.

A modestly but well-dressed woman in her forties, color-treated hair tastefully styled, makeup expertly applied to accent her eyes, undoubtedly her best feature.

Noting the stack of files beside her computer and on the credenza behind her, Paul attempted to strike up a conversation. "Looks like they keep you pretty busy."

Her reply was forthright but cordial. "We're used to hearing the complaint that government is bloated, too big a budget to accomplish too little of what constituents want. But we're actually understaffed here at City Hall; most of us do the work of two people. We haven't had a raise for several years, especially with the housing slump and the resulting loss of property tax revenue."

"How long have you worked for the City?"

"Twelve years, the last four with Mr. White here in Planning. Before that, I was in the Finance Department."

"I would imagine Planning to be more interesting than Finance."

"You probably think that because your clients are real estate developers. But yes, I've found working with Mr. White to be rewarding. He's smart, congenial, and politically savvy. We make a good team." She couldn't hide the pride in her voice. "He tells people I'm the nuts and bolts behind his genius."

Do I detect a hint of entitlement in the way she speaks about her relationship with the Director?

"You mentioned the amount of work. Does it require working past regular office hours?"

"I don't mind working long hours. I have no family of my own; I have the time available. But it doesn't usually mean extra money. The budget has minimal provision for paying overtime."

"Does the Director work overtime as well?"

"He puts in his fair share. Of course, he's at a much higher pay grade so he's more than adequately compensated. Enough, in fact, that he and his wife recently returned from a cruise to the Bahamas." There was no mistaking a trace of bitterness in her voice.

"Doesn't working late wreak havoc on his family life? My wife reacts even when I don't make it home in time for dinner."

"The Director's home life is in a habitual state of havoc."

Surprised by her candor, Paul continued to probe: "Because he spends so much time at work?"

158

"Because nothing he does for his wife is good enough. She's always complaining. About his job, wanting a larger house, a newer car, more money to spend."

"That makes for an unhappy marriage. Has he considered divorce?"

Marcia snickered. "She'd take him to the cleaners. He finds it easier to tune her out and find diversion elsewhere."

I wonder how long Marcia's been his diversion. Has she realized Charles White can't or won't deliver what she wants from a relationship?

Am I sitting across from the source of the leak to the police about the Director? She said she doesn't report overtime. She may have been working late the night Tom's office received the anonymous tip but there's probably no record of it.

At that instant, the subject of the conversation walked through the door. "Not speaking out of school, are we, Marcia?" His tone sounded friendly, but his eyes threw daggers.

Without further regard for her, he approached Paul and shook hands vigorously. The grip was strong but the palms were moist.

"Good to see you, Paul. Please come in."

Marcia was right about his being politically savvy. Score a point for him: Remembering my name.

The Director led the way into his office, calling to Marcia for two coffees.

Charles White was a big man, broad-shouldered, with a belly beginning to expand over his belt. He had a long face with a thin chin, wide distance between the eyes, and a large prolonged nose: the facial traits of a higher IQ, confirming Marcia's assessment. Thread veins around his nose suggested rosacea or fondness for an evening cocktail or two.

After spending several moments with prerequisite pleasantries, the Director looked at his watch. "What can I help you with, Paul?"

159

Score two for him: Taking control by letting me know he's a busy man. I need to throw him a curve to establish equilibrium.

"You're aware of the murder at the Pier."

"Of course. Big news for our little town." Charles leaned back in his chair resting his arms across his stomach, appearing relaxed. But his eyes were once again at odds with his words, narrowing into slits of wariness.

"The police approached me about possible irregularities in Neal's business dealings. Knowing of my real estate consultancy, they felt I might be able to lend insight into activities prior to his death."

"What kind of irregularities?"

"They examined his bank statements and found large, unexplained cash withdrawals."

"That's some kind of cloak and dagger material, Paul." His voice dripped sarcasm. "But what does it have to do with your reason for coming to see me?"

"You didn't let me finish. The police are looking into Neal's recent activities with the Planning Department."

Score one for me: Throw your opponent off guard.

For a large man, he moved swiftly to close the door. It was too late. From the expression on Marcia's face, she had overheard the conversation.

Those two will have a lot to talk about at their after-hours session tonight.

"Is there a point to all this?" His voice sounded impatient, with an undertone of anxiety.

"They haven't been able to locate the plans Neal should have resubmitted to get Final Permits on his last two projects."

"Maybe he never got Final Permits."

"Oh, he got them alright. I checked Public Records myself. The revised Plans should be on file as well. No one has been able to find them."

"What information did the police want from you?" Beads of perspiration appeared on his forehead.

"They asked how Neal could get Final Permits if the Plans rejected by the City Council had never been revised and resubmitted."

The Director tried to recover his composure. "I'm sure our Department will be able to locate the revised Plans. With the amount of paperwork that flows through Planning, things get misplaced from time to time. Thankfully, it doesn't happen often. I'll make sure our clerks look more diligently for the missing Plans."

Score two for me: Put your opponent on the defensive. He's making excuses and false promises. He's attempting to place blame on an incompetent staff, but he has no intention of having his clerks waste time looking for something they can't possibly find.

"Surely, this isn't what you came to discuss," he continued, making a point of looking at his watch again. "Marcia said you made the appointment to discuss Plans one of your clients is submitting."

"Actually, my visit's in the same context of what we're talking about. If Neal was, in fact, able to get Plan Approval without resubmitting Plans, it appears there have been changes in Plan requirements. I have a responsibility to my clients to stay on top of any new policies and procedures." Paul let the words hang in the air. "I'm sure you understand my need to assure my clients that all developers are treated equally in the process."

The sunlight filtering through the window was blocked as the man rose to his full height. "There have been no changes in Plan requirements."

His hospitality has worn thin. No cordial use of my first name now.

The Director walked around his desk and opened the door, leaving no doubt the meeting had concluded.

"I think you've been subjected to a vast overreaction on the part of someone at police headquarters. I'm certain no evidence will be found of irregular behavior of any kind by Neal Henderson. After all, don't forget he represents Don Carson, the biggest developer in the County. Don would never allow a dishonest man to rise to Neal's rank in his organization."

"I'm sure Neal wasn't dishonest when he started working for Don. All of us are subject to financial pressures of raising a family, maintaining expensive lifestyles, and living up to other people's expectations. Men don't start out dishonest as much as they become less and less honest over time. Their integrity dissolves as their ideals are subjected to a slow process of erosion."

Charles put a hand on Paul's shoulder walking him to Marcia's desk.

"Thanks for coming in, Paul. My secretary will see you out." He returned to his office and closed the door without looking back.

Chapter Seventeen

Tom stopped at the chocolate shop on his way to meet with the Councilwoman. The girl behind the counter offered him a sample of a chocolate truffle. "Delicious. Give me a small box of those."

Watching her box the confection and wrap a bow around the box, he considered getting a box for Maddy. Maybe it would restore him in her good graces. As usual, he had no idea what had angered her or what he should be making amends for. He sometimes felt on more solid ground dealing with criminals. At least he could halfway predict their behavior.

Arriving at the appointed time, he saw the interior office was empty.

"Don't worry," Rosemary assured him. "She's not standing you up; she's been delayed. She should be here in ten or fifteen minutes."

Tom wasn't surprised. He figured the Councilwoman would be late for their meeting as part of her game of one-upmanship.

He leaned over the secretary's desk, handing her the box of sweets. "Put those in your desk where she won't see them."

She wagged her finger as if scolding him. "Why, Detective, are you bribing me?"

Interesting choice of words, Tom thought to himself. *Is she letting me know she was the person behind the anonymous tip about the Planning Director?*

He observed her carefully but her expression gave nothing away. "Certainly not, Ma'am. Appreciative of all your hard work here at City Hall, that's all."

Tom took a seat to await Mrs. Patton's arrival. Certain Neal Henderson and Margaret Patton had an affair, he considered the best approach to get her to disclose their relationship without putting her on the defensive.

What hot buttons can I press?

What was her interest in Neal? A whimsical fling, a mutually beneficial arrangement, an alternative for a loveless marriage?

What had attracted Neal to the Councilwoman? He had been on the brink of getting married to a lovely woman, his high school sweetheart. What did Mrs. Patton have to offer that enticed him enough to break off his engagement?

The three things most important to Neal appeared to be women, power, and money. Margaret Patton provided two of those elements. Had she provided all three?

Tom walked to the window and looked at the hills surrounding City Hall. He pursed his lower lip between his fingers, deep in thought.

Had their relationship soured? Had it put her job, her reputation, or her marriage in jeopardy?

What about the picture of her in the hot tub at his apartment? Had Neal used the picture to blackmail her?

With more than enough motive, the Councilwoman was becoming more than a person of interest in this case. She was rapidly becoming the prime suspect.

Tom answered his cell. "Hey, man." Seeing Rosemary Hanson glance toward him, he was careful not to reveal the name of his caller.

"Can you talk?" Paul asked.

"Go ahead. I'm waiting for an appointment." He threw a smile in the secretary's direction and she turned back to her work.

"I made a trip to the Planning Department after our little talk. Fortunately, the woman I know was working the front counter for walk-ins. I used the subterfuge of working on a new project for a client who would soon be submitting Plans for the Council's approval. Asked if there had been any recent changes or rulings I should know about that might affect my client's outcome."

"Good approach."

"She told me the only plans she had recently seen rejected were for floor space ratios and height requirements not being met per Code.

'Not one of my client's Plans, I hope.' I said to her.

'Oh, no,' she responded. 'As I recall, it was one of Mr. Henderson's projects. Victoria Square, I think. I hadn't thought about it since the terrible thing that happened to him.' I commiserated with her."

"All fine and dandy, Paul. But how is it helpful to me?"

"In itself, it's not. But her answer when I asked if the Plans passed when they were resubmitted might be of more interest to you."

"Don't keep me in suspense, buddy."

"She looked a little baffled, then shook her head. 'Now that you mention it, I saw Plan Approvals in the file but there were no new Plans submitted.' "

"Bingo. That's what I wanted to hear. Did she give any explanation as to how that could happen?"

"She had a call come in. I told her to take the call, thanked her, and left. I didn't want to push the issue and possibly get her in trouble in case she started asking questions."

"Good move. Exactly what I would have done. I want to wait for the perfect opportunity to tip our hand."

"When do you think that might occur?"

Tom saw Margaret Patton walking in from the parking lot. "I think it's arriving now through the back doors of City Hall."

* * *

Hurrying through the outer office, the Councilwoman acknowledged her secretary with a curt nod and called to Tom over her shoulder as she passed through to her inner sanctum. "Give me a minute, Detective."

No apology for being late, Tom noted.

Rosemary looked at Tom and shrugged her shoulders. He gave her a wink.

It was more than several minutes before she called: "Please come in, Detective."

Whatever business she had attended to was not obvious. There were no files on her desk; no briefcase in sight. *Is she meticulous, or secretive?*

She wasted no time on cordialities. Arrogance was apparent from the smirk on her face but her constant finger tapping belied her self-assurance. "I can't imagine what questions you have for me about Neal Henderson. I hardly knew the man."

In a split second, Tom decided against diplomacy. If this woman wanted to play games, he could play hardball, too. He went right for the jugular.

Pulling out the picture of her with Neal in the hot tub, he threw it on the desk in front of her.

"That would suggest differently."

She blanched. Her eyes narrowed to slits. He could almost see her wheels turning.

In the brief silence, they could both hear fingers flying across a keyboard. She stood and walked around the desk. Gingerly picking up the corner of the picture between her thumb and forefinger, she handed it back to Tom on her way to close the office door.

By the time she resumed her seat, she had collected herself. Steepling her hands in front of her, she looked smug and in control as she responded.

"I'm not saying there are things I've done I'd rather not be made public, but I have nothing to hide that would be of interest to you."

"Oh, to the contrary. I think you're at the heart of my entire investigation."

Her lips became thinner and the corners of her mouth turned down in an unattractive manner. "I beg to differ with you, Detective. It sounds to me like you're attributing more to my involvement with Neal Henderson than it warrants."

"Please feel free to enlighten me on the error of my assumptions." He let the sarcasm drip off his tongue in an effort to rattle her.

She sighed, leaned back in her chair and raised her hands in front of her, palms up. "So I had a fling with the egotistic heel. Why is it of interest to you?"

"Were you the reason he broke off his engagement?"

"I seriously doubt it. Neal had visions of who he wanted to be and where he wanted to go. His plans didn't include being hampered by a high school sweetheart who wanted to start a family."

"And your reason for becoming involved with Neal?"

"Let me help you get a clearer picture, Detective," she sighed impatiently. "My husband and I have interests that have diverged in recent years. He's become consumed with his roses and his dogs. That's fine with me; I'm happy he's found hobbies which amuse him."

Do I detect the same contempt she seems to have for everyone else?

"My interests lie in the public sector. I met Mr. Henderson in the course of my dealings with local businessmen. We found we had things in common which we shared over a few late night dinners."

Tom's pulse jumped a beat but he maintained a neutral expression. "Wouldn't that relationship be considered a conflict of interest considering your position and the developer he represented?"

167

For the first time, Tom detected a chink in her armor as she squirmed slightly. "We were discrete. I didn't let our relationship influence any of my actions on the Council."

Tom hoped his next punch would be a knockout blow. "I beg to differ with you, Councilwoman. We have information there was collusion between you, the Planning Director, and Neal Henderson."

"Stop right there, Detective," she warned. Her voice was low pitched and threatening. "You're getting perilously close to exposing yourself to a defamation of character lawsuit."

How many times have I been the recipient of the same threat from suspects perilously close to discovery? Unabashed, he continued his verbal assault: "We found the first leg in the tripod when we accessed Neal's bank records. With that evidence, we'll be able to obtain warrants for the Director's financial records as well as your own. It shouldn't be too difficult to trace any pay-for-play exchanges."

The crows' feet at the corners of her eyes became more pronounced as her brows furrowed. The corners of her mouth sagged. The high-handedness of her earlier demeanor was gradually being replaced by fear. Tom knew he was winning.

"My only involvement with Neal and Charles White was to arrange a meeting. Until then, Neal's only dealings with the Planning Department had been with staff members. I've known the Director for years. I simply arranged an introduction for the two of them over cocktails. We met at the hotel, had a rather inane conversation, and I left. They decided to have dinner at the hotel's restaurant."

She inspected her fingernails, trying to appear relaxed and bored. "I had no part in whatever the two of them may have cooked up between them."

"What reason did Neal give for wanting an introduction to the Director?"

"I assumed it was part of his relentless pursuit of success. He had grandiose notions of himself as the successor to Don Carson's empire. Frankly, I doubt it ever would have happened. Neal lacked Don's integrity, charisma, and people skills."

"Do you think he would have pursued illegal methods to ensure his success?"

"Of course." The bluntness of the reply caught Tom off guard.

She acknowledged his surprise with a dismissive wave of her hand. "The man lacked the moral barometer most of us have, the one that saves us from ourselves. He didn't know when to stop, where to draw the line."

"What about Charles White? Was he capable of complicity with Neal?"

Her eyebrows arched as she gave careful consideration before replying. "From what I've seen of Charles over the years, his moral barometer is intact but he has his weaknesses."

"Can you clarify?"

She picked a piece of lint from her sleeve. "He's married to a woman who is somewhat of a shrew. She can make his life miserable if he doesn't accommodate her every whim."

"Would it make him vulnerable to financial influences?"

"I can't say, Detective."

"Can't or won't?" Tom was losing patience with her cavalier attitude.

"Oh, I'm not refraining from throwing Charles White under the bus out any sense of loyalty. I simply don't know the answer to your question."

Her response might have seemed nonchalant were it not for the intensity of her eyes. "All I'm suggesting is he has his weaknesses if someone had an interest in exploiting them."

He finished the thought. "Someone like Neal Henderson."

"Those are your words, not mine."

Tom knew when it was fruitless to pursue a particular line of questioning. Besides, as he told Paul earlier, he wasn't interested in possible charges of bribery or collusion. It was time to stop pulling punches.

He shifted in his chair, leaning forward. "I don't want to take any more of your time than is necessary, Councilwoman. I know you're a busy woman."

Her shoulders rounded as the tension dissipated. The finger tapping stopped. "I appreciate your concern." She imitated his smile with a weak one of her own, realizing too late the direction the conversation was taking.

"Besides, bribery isn't my area of expertise. I'm sure if any allegations of misconduct arise, the District Attorney will be more than eager to bring charges, especially with an election year looming."

Her look changed instantly to one of venom.

"So let's get to the real reason for my visit."

The finger tapping started again accompanied by a clicking of her shoe against the desk.

"Uncovering the reason for Neal Henderson's brutal murder, and ultimately, of course, the identity of the murderer."

Her reaction was one of outrage though whether it was real or feigned, Tom couldn't be sure.

"You aren't seriously suggesting I killed Neal Henderson?" Her eyes bore into his as the color in her face darkened.

"You had sufficient motive. Whether or not you were complicit in his dealings with the Planning Department, he was becoming a threat to your elected position as well as a threat to your marriage. Unless, of course, you and your husband have an open marriage arrangement."

"We most certainly do not and I deeply resent the implication."

Her pretense of indignation amused Tom. "Or was it anger and humiliation over being used by a social climbing status seeker that finally brought you to a boiling point and got the best of you?"

She put a hand to her mouth, pinching her lower lip. The silence in the room was palpable. After what seemed moments but was probably mere seconds, she clutched both hands in front of her.

"You're right about one thing. I did end up despising the bastard." She moved her head from side to side as if shaking off painful memories. "If he wouldn't have ended it, I would have. It was like watching an out of control train racing down the track. You knew at some point, it was going to derail. Once I came to my senses, I realized how much I had to lose. I didn't want to crash with him."

For the first time in their conversation, he felt she was being honest, willing to expose her vulnerability at great expense to her pride. He waited for the other shoe to fall.

"But I didn't kill him."

"Where were you Monday night between seven and nine o'clock?" Tom pressed, hoping his prime suspect didn't have an alibi for the time of the murder.

"You can check with my assistant. I was a hundred and twenty miles away at a seminar on government affairs."

The irony of the subject matter escaped neither of them.

Still, Tom was accepting nothing at face value from this woman. "You may have made plans to attend a seminar but can anyone confirm you were actually in attendance?"

"Approximately two hundred people, Detective," she answered, tilting her head arrogantly, lips parted in a tight, thin line. "I was the main speaker."

Chapter Eighteen

Scott drove through Seagate to Maddy's house. Calling on the premise of retrieving his kerchief, he had received an invitation to dinner.

Designated parking spots were narrow, leaving little room for cars to pass his four-by-four. Lot setbacks were minimal and yards were small. *How do people live so close to each other? I need to be surrounded by wide open space.*

The splash of color he met walking through the picket fence gate stopped him in his tracks: red and yellow roses, blue lily-of-the-Nile, and purplish fuchsia. Irises, sunflowers, and daisies bloomed on the path leading to the porch. Potted plants flanking the entry were warm and welcoming.

The front door was ajar. Scot followed the instruction of a wood carved sign hanging on the screen. 'Come in and give a holler.'

"Maddy?" The aroma of meat sizzling on a grill filled his nostrils, making his mouth water.

"I'm in the kitchen, Scott. Make yourself comfortable. I'll be right out."

Looking around, he was relieved and pleasantly surprised. With her skill and expertise in design, he had expected chic modern furnishings which he considered uncomfortable and dysfunctional. Instead, the room was furnished in a cheerful, relaxing nautical style. A sand colored sofa and side chairs were set off with blue and tan striped pillows. Candles and seashells in clear jars accented a built-in bookcase. The focal point of the room was an eye-catching painting of sailboats covering the large wall. A series of framed navigational maps were artfully arranged on the smaller walls.

Maddy whisked into the room pulling an apron over her head and brushing her hair back with a forearm. Small beads of perspiration showed on her upper lip.

"Okay. Everything's prepared. Now, we can relax while the ribs cook themselves to perfection. I use a marinade that's my own special concoction. I think you'll like it."

"If it ends up tasting anything like it smells, it'll be amazing."

"We can walk down to the park while the meat's cooking if you like. Our timing should be right to see a beautiful sunset."

* * *

Scott stole glances of Maddy as they walked. The sleeveless short dress she wore accented her flawless skin and shapely long legs. Her smile was gentle and sweet. Her hair was smooth and silky making him want to reach out and touch it to see how it felt in his hand.

But it was more than her beauty that affected him. It was how comfortable she seemed. He couldn't imagine her being in a situation where she felt awkward or out of place. A sense of self radiated from her whatever setting she was in. Even in Roberto's clutches, she had displayed her own brand of sauciness.

The field in the center of the park was crowded with lawn chairs, makeshift volleyball nets, and mini soccer posts. They followed the walking path along the shore onto the jetty. Sitting on flat rocks at the end, they gazed across the endless ocean to the outline of islands on the horizon.

They sat in silence, listening to waves lapping against the shore, seagulls squawking, and children laughing. Scott filled his lungs with the clean, fresh air and ran his hands through his hair, made curly by the saltwater spray.

The sun was beginning to set. Oranges, pinks, reds, and yellows overpowered the blue sky. The reflection of the glowing ball expanded in the water as the sun dropped toward the horizon.

"It's easy to see why you like living close to the ocean."

"I can't imagine not being able to see it every day. I feel like it's a source of energy." She picked up a handful of sand, letting it trail through her fingers. "I love the neighborhood because of its sense of community and relaxed, resort style of living."

"I like the painting on your living room wall. Do you sail?"

"Lea and I grew up in San Diego. Our dad was a cop. When he got time off, which wasn't often, he took us sailing. His dream was to sail to South America when he retired. Unfortunately, he had a stroke before he could make that voyage. His activities are limited now. He still insists on being taken out on his boat from time to time but he no longer mans the helm."

"Are you close to your father?"

"Very. Both Maddy and I adore him. Paul teases me and my sister that we inherited his sleuthing instinct but not his skill."

"What kind of father was he growing up?"

"Strict, but fair. He was tougher on me as the first born, and because I caused more problems. Lea was the good daughter. Grades, behavior, everything she did was good, except sports. I was more of a rebel. I'm afraid you were right in pegging me as a handful. That reputation goes way back. School bored me. Without sports, I probably would have played hooky most of the time. I was adventurous, lived outside the box. Mom always told me I was the daughter more like Dad but he wouldn't admit it."

"You and I have that in common."

"What do you mean?"

"It was the same in our family. My sister was the level-headed one who did everything our father asked of her. I had my own ideas about how things should be done and how I should live my life."

174

"Is that why you left?"

"So you heard my story."

"Paul learned about your family when a client tried to buy some land from your grandfather."

"I'm sure Granddad didn't sell."

"You're right. He told Paul he was keeping the Ranch intact for his grandson."

"I was never planning to return. Paul's client may have eventually ended up with that land except for what happened."

Maddy waited, not wanting to intrude if Scott chose not to discuss the tragedy. He rubbed his hands together forming a steeple with his fingers where he rested his chin.

"A major life event can turn a person inside out. Who you were disappears. You become a different person. What happened that night in Colorado is a piece of who I am now. It's a piece of who my daughter is."

"It must have been terrible for your little girl."

"Yeah." He turned away, looking at the sunset. "I was almost incapable of coping myself. Trying to help a five-year-old understand what had happened was the worst experience of my life.

Until then, I hadn't thought much about death. My father had passed, but I was miles away when it happened; I wasn't surrounded with the grief of his dying. With the invincibility of youth, I considered my own demise an event so far in the future it didn't bear thinking about.

But I had to come to grips with my notion of what death is all about in order to give my daughter the comfort she needed. To do that, I tried to see things through her eyes. In a mysterious way, I found my own comfort by using a child's perspective.

I remembered losing my dog when I was in grade school. Knowing how attached I was to that dog, my parents worried about how to help me through the pain. But I knew the dog loved me too much to let my heart break by leaving me. He communicated with me in a way I can't explain to let me know I hadn't lost him; he'd just taken on a different form. Somehow, I knew his spirit was inside me; he was part of who I am. I let my daughter know her mom was in her the same way; part of who she is and always will be.

He picked up some stones and skipped them across the water. "When you go through a transformative event like that, you feel like you're walking in somebody else's shoes; like the life you worked so hard to create doesn't fit anymore. You try to find meaning in life; try to make sense of your experience. It can completely change the direction of the path you've chosen."

"For the better?"

"I don't know that there's a better or a worse to how our lives turn out. It's all part of something much bigger than us at work. I think a person's journey is designed to teach things we're sent here to learn. Life teaches us those things in the end, one way or another."

"Is that why you decided to move back home to the Ranch?"

"When I saw how short our time here can be, I realized what a waste it was to be separated from loved ones over differences of opinion."

A shiver ran up Maddy's spine.

"I don't know why I told you all this. It's something I don't much talk about."

She smiled gently as he stood up, pulling her to her feet.

"Let's get you home. It's getting chilly. I can already taste those ribs."

* * *

Scott enjoyed the leisurely pace of the dinner, savoring each tasty bite. Their conversation was the comfortable kind of people who have known each other a long time.

Pushing back from the picnic table, he ran his hands over his belly. "I feel like I'm bursting at the seams. Your homemade apple pie finished me off. Let me work some of this off by helping with the dishes."

Once again, he surprised her, not only carrying the dishes into the kitchen but rolling up his sleeves and washing as she dried.

He moved to the living room while she blew out candles in the back yard. He eased himself into a side chair putting his hands behind his head. Visions of how the night might end crowded his thoughts. Were his feelings running deeper than he had anticipated?

Immediately following his wife's death, he'd run the gamut of emotions: denial, anger, depression, guilt. He eventually shut down emotionally, not allowing himself to have any feelings.

In the months following his return to the Ranch, his grandfather had helped him heal by telling him to honor his wife's life, not her death. He reminded his grandson that when his wife was alive, they had shared laughter, joy, and life. She would want Scott and their daughter to live that way now.

In the last few days, Scott had become aware of how much he missed sharing things with a woman: family outings, horseback riding, hiking, cooking, holidays. But the last thing he wanted was any kind of emotional entanglement. He wanted a friendship, nothing more.

Maddy seemed like a perfect fit: intelligent, outgoing, fun. Her beauty was a plus, but not a prerequisite for Scott. She would make a wonderful friend and a woman his daughter would take to.

The problem was he was already wondering if he'd be able to keep his feelings in check with this captivating woman. Was he kidding himself that he could keep things light with her?

Like the houses on either side of Maddy, he felt things closing in. He needed to back off. He needed space.

"After dinner drink?" Maddy asked, entering the room.

"Sorry, no, I've got to go. The dinner was delicious. I can't reciprocate with the cooking, but I'd like you to come up to see the Ranch sometime. I'll call you and we'll set something up."

Standing in the middle of the room watching the screen door close behind him, Maddy wondered exactly where she stood.

Chapter Nineteen

Maddy was pruning her rose bushes when Lea pulled into her driveway and called out. "How was dinner last night?"

"It was fine. But I'll admit, I can't quite figure out where I am with that man."

"Where do you want to be with him?"

"Haven't figured that out either. Why are you here anyway?"

"Checking to see what you're doing today."

Maddy approached the car with mild curiosity. "I haven't made up my mind yet. What do you have in mind?"

"Paul talked to Tom at their softball game last night. Tom has checked the Councilwoman off his list of suspects."

"Why?"

"Apparently, she has a rock solid alibi for the time of the murder."

"Too bad. I know you liked her as a suspect because she turned down your bid," Maddy responded snidely.

"That's not the reason." Lea sounded hurt, although she had to admit there was probably some truth to what her sister said. "I don't care what Tom thinks; Gracie's never wrong. She had some reason to be so agitated by the Councilwoman and her bodyguard. We need to look into it. You need to talk to her husband and see what you can find out.

Maddy pointed at herself. "Me, why me?"

"Because Mrs. Patton and her bodyguard both know me. If I was caught at her house, I could get in real trouble."

"So I should be willing to get in trouble to keep you out of trouble?" Maddy complained.

"Come on, Mad. You're always good at creating plausible reasons for your snooping."

Maddy took exception to Lea's choice of words: "When you do it, it's called detecting. When I do it, it's called snooping."

Lea paid little attention to her sister's protests. She knew what she suggested was exactly the kind of challenge her sister relished.

Maddy's eyes drifted to the sky. "I suppose I could ask Mr. Patton for pictures of his famous rose garden for our home furnishings publication."

Lea gave a thumbs up. "Great idea. While you're at the house, you might get an opportunity to find out more about Max."

Maddy puckered her nose and lips. "Why would I want to do that?"

"Because he's one of Gracie's prime suspects."

* * *

Arriving at the Patton's hillside country home, Maddy smelled the sweet fragrance of lilacs as she drove through the iron gates and parked in the circular driveway. The door was answered by an older Hispanic woman, drying her hands on a towel as she dusted flour from her apron.

She smiled broadly. "Mr. Patton told me to expect you. He's in his rose garden. I'll show you the way."

Maddy gasped as they walked through the main house. It had an open floor plan with walls of sliding glass doors on three sides providing unobstructed views of the surrounding mountains and valleys, all the way to the ocean. Her head rotated taking in the colorful wall paintings and sculptures showcased in niches and alcoves throughout the rooms.

"Beautiful, isn't it?" the housekeeper asked over her shoulder. "The view always takes people's breath away on their first visit."

Maddy clasped her hands to her throat. "I think it would take my breath away every day I lived here."

180

Moving outside, they passed a lap pool overlooking acres of fruit and avocado trees. The pungent smell of chlorine mixed with the intoxicating smell of orange blossoms. They continued along a path bordered by rosemary, iris, and oleander, the plants brushing against Maddy's skin.

Entering under an archway, they entered a garden overflowing with roses of all colors: whites, yellows, reds, pinks, and purples. Maddy's senses were engulfed in the fragrances of jasmine and rosemary, and the sweet sound of songbirds.

"Mr. Patton. Your guest has arrived."

The man who turned to greet her was as handsome as she remembered from seeing one of his live performances at the local theatre. His almost wrinkle-free skin and erect posture belied his age. The gray streaking his hair only served to augment his good looks.

"Please come in. Did you have any trouble finding us?"

"None at all. It's all so beautiful . . . the drive here, your house, this garden."

"Yes, we feel blessed to be surrounded by so much beauty. And now, more beauty has come into my day."

Maddy blushed, finding herself somewhat tongue-tied in the presence of his charisma.

"Please, make yourself comfortable," he invited, indicating a glass-topped wood table surrounded by driftwood wicker chairs. The cushions of vibrant yellow lent a splash of color accented by an overhead umbrella.

"I appreciate your letting us use this lovely garden as a backdrop for the displays in our furniture publication."

"My wife and I are more than happy to open our garden to you. I'm glad of the opportunity to share the beauty of these flowers with your readers."

The housekeeper returned with a pitcher of iced tea and thick slices of pound cake which she set in front of them. They talked about furniture, artwork, and gardening. Maddy waited for an opportunity to broach the other topic she had come to discuss.

Placing her empty plate aside, she sat back. "You've certainly been blessed with a green thumb. Does your wife share your enthusiasm for gardening?"

The moment he placed the linen napkin across his plate, the housekeeper magically reappeared to remove their plates and refill their glasses. He smiled at her. "Thank you, Rosa. Your cake was delicious, as always."

He turned back to answer the question. "Margaret? No. My wife appreciates the beauty of the flowers, but her only interest beyond how they look lies in arranging them as centerpieces for our dinner parties."

He smiled impishly. "It's a good thing because I confess to being a little selfish in that regard. I insist on doing all my own planting and tending. I let the gardener take care of the grounds but the garden is off limits to everyone but me. I've even concocted my own home remedies for the pests that attack my roses. Quite effective, I might add."

"I'll have to get your recipe sometime. I take pride in my own gardening skills. I certainly outshine my sister in that regard, but that's not hard to do. My problem is I lack the space to keep much gardening equipment on hand. I have one small shed stacked to the roof with pots and small tools."

"I'm fortunate to have all the room I need for my gardening paraphernalia. Margaret complains I've got my own mini version of a garden store in our back yard."

"Your wife must be busy with her community involvement."

"Yes. Margaret and I live rather separate lives now that I've retired. She's taken over all the charitable and community activities. I'm content showing my dogs and growing my roses. Of course, I'm very proud of her service on the City Council. She may even seek further office on the state level someday."

The man looked off toward the ocean and for the first time, Maddy could see the wrinkles around his eyes. But he displayed no signs of regret or longing. *He does, indeed, seem to be a contented man, at peace with himself and his surroundings.*

"Is it only the two of you living here?"

"We're fortunate our children are close. They bring the grandchildren for frequent visits. And, of course, I have Max."

Bingo.

"Another grandchild?" she inquired innocently.

He laughed. "Hardly. Max is our driver and bodyguard. He's been with me since the beginning of my acting career, through all the ups and downs. I can't imagine life without him. When I had this house built, I made sure the architect included a small house for Max right here on the property. Same style as the main house. Complete with his own TV room, workout area, and kitchen. We call it Max's Place."

"How did you and Max find each other?"

"A director recommended him to me. Max was an unemployed Vet with no family who was doing odd jobs at the studio. The skills he learned in the military carried over into his service for me. There's nothing he can't or won't do for me, and his loyalty is impeccable. Of course, I'm not so much in need of his services now that I'm retired. Much of his time is devoted to driving my wife around town."

The housekeeper announced the arrival of another visitor. Maddy stood to leave, extending her hand. "Thank you again for opening up your beautiful garden to us."

Rather than shaking her hand, the older gentleman turned it downward, gracing it with a kiss. "It's been my pleasure, Maddy. We'll see you soon with your photographer in tow."

* * *

Maddy followed the walkway from the garden through an archway leading to the veranda. Walking toward the circular drive where her car was parked, she noticed a small courtyard adjacent to the main house. Stopping to admire the fountain, she saw a guest house, the exterior closely matching the design of the main building.

Looks like the cottage Art described where Max lives. Can't hurt to take a look.

She was squinting her eyes to peer into the windows when a hand on her shoulder made her jump. "May I help you with something, Ma'am?"

Spinning around, she gave the man a quick once-over. From the muscular torso and the bulging cords in his neck, she didn't have to guess who was asking.

Her breath quickened. Smiling innocently, she offered an explanation close enough to the truth if he tried to confirm it with his boss. "Mr. Patton told me to look around for other locations we can use for our photography shoot."

The bodyguard began to move closer when a man's voice behind him interceded.

"It's alright, Max. She's with me."

Taking her by the hand, Tom steered Maddy out of the courtyard before she had a chance to object. Max turned abruptly and returned to the guest house.

"Not very sociable is he?" Maddy observed haughtily.

Moving briskly, Tom pulled her to her car. "I'm here on official police business. Would you care to tell me why you're here?" He peered over his sunglasses, waiting for an explanation.

"I'm here on official furniture store business," she replied defiantly, chin jutting in the air. She removed his hand from her elbow. "Anyway, how do you know Max?"

Tom opened the car door and leaned against it, motioning for her to sit down. "He's had a couple of run-ins with the law.

Nothing serious. Mostly incidents of his keeping autograph enthusiasts away from his boss."

He massaged the back of his neck, looking at her sternly: "Let's get back to you. Why do I find your being here on furniture store business a coincidence more than a little hard to swallow?"

"Believe what you will, Tom." She toyed with a lock of hair. "But why are you here on police business? I thought you told Paul the Councilwoman was no longer a suspect."

"Not that it's any of your business, but I'm interviewing Mr. Patton as an investor in Don Carson's luxury housing project. Thought he may have had occasion to deal with Neal and could give me his impression of the deceased."

Maddy clapped her hands. "Oh, I get it. That's the cover you're using to find out if he knew of his wife's affair."

Tom didn't know whether to admire Maddy's cleverness or worry about Art Patton reading him as easily as she had. He pulled his notepad from his pocket.

"At least I learned one thing from your incorrigible meddling."

She raised an eyebrow. "Which is?"

"When Max put his hand on your shoulder, he reached with his left hand." He scribbled on the pad. "He's left-handed."

Maddy's voice took on a hint of intrigue. "I can give you another bit of useful information."

"What would that be?"

"Mr. Patton's got enough gardening equipment to open a mini nursery." She looked pleased with her revelation.

"Are you suggesting he was the one at Neal's condo disguised as an exterminator?"

"I'm saying there are plenty of bug sprayers here. I admit; he hardly looks the part, but Max does. And remember, Mr. Patton's an actor. He's an expert at adopting disguises and playing roles."

Maddy hesitated, caught up in her theory. "Except the guard at Neal's condo said the intruder was wearing something with a bug emblem on it. I'm sure they don't keep uniforms like that here."

"People see what they want to see, Maddy," Tom suggested. "What the guard described as a bug may have been a Karate badge."

Maddy's eyes widened. "Does that mean you're looking into Max, too? Is he a suspect?"

"I'm looking into everyone who has even a remote connection to this case."

"Why, Tom," she asked playfully, "am I on your list?"

He scoffed. "Oh, you're always on my list, Maddy. Which list you're on varies from one week to the next."

Tom jotted another note on his pad and returned it to his shirt pocket. Slamming her car door, he straightened. "You need to go before Max wonders what we're standing out here jawing about, but thanks for sharing."

"You can thank me later," she added suggestively, "at a more suitable time and place."

He walked toward the main house scratching his head.

Chapter Twenty

Art Patton greeted Tom with an outstretched hand, a smile playing on his lips.

"Come in, Detective. Welcome. You're my second visitor already today. Quite a busy day I'm having."

He spread his arms, indicating a chair where Tom could sit across from him. Tom sensed the older man was fishing for something. *Had he seen me talking with Maddy?*

"Yes, I saw Maddy on my way in."

"You two know each other?"

He recognized the need to be honest and direct with this man. "We're friends. She told me about doing a layout in your garden for her furniture store. She's quite excited."

"I'm looking forward to it as well."

He's charming, alright.

"May I offer you refreshment, Detective?" he asked as the housekeeper entered. "A bite to eat?"

Tom rejected the ploy to turn the interview into a social situation. "No, thanks. I'll try to keep this as brief as possible so I don't take too much of your time."

The older man smiled but sat erect in his chair, alert and wary. He crossed his legs and folded his hands in his lap. "Fire away, then. How may I be of assistance?"

"I spoke with your wife at City Hall yesterday. Are you aware of our conversation?"

"As a matter of fact, she came to me shortly after you interviewed her. She was quite upset. Admitted she had done something stupid; something she wasn't proud of. She didn't want to keep it bottled inside any longer because she was afraid it would come between us."

"What had I asked that had her so worried?"

"Oh, it wasn't anything you said that frightened her. Your conversation simply made her come to her senses. She realized if you had found out about her indiscretion, other people probably knew or would find out as well. Eventually, it would get back to me. Buena Viaje is a small town, Detective, especially when it comes to gossip. Once the word got out, it would have spread like wildfire."

"And she didn't want it ruining her reputation."

"It wasn't her reputation she was worried about. She didn't want it ruining our marriage."

Tom's face displayed skepticism, but Art continued anyway. "There was more to it than that. I found something out about my wife last night I hadn't known. She told me how much she has come to hate politics. The longer she's been in office, the more she sees government as petty game-playing for power at the expense of the public whose money and freedoms are being exchanged for services they would prefer to do without."

"That's a fairly stringent condemnation of politics."

"I thought so, too," he chuckled, "but one with which I concur. In fact, she had decided not to run again. She was afraid to tell me for fear I'd be disappointed in her."

"And would you?"

"Be disappointed in her? To the contrary. What Margaret has never fully accepted in all the years we've been married is that I'm happy with whatever makes her happy. If it's politics, fine. If it's climbing Mt. Everest, fine. If it's having her own business, that's fine, too. In fact, that's what we've decided she should do. She's going back to her roots in catering and starting her own catering business right here in Buena Viaje."

Interesting, Tom thought, *but not what I've come for. It's time to tackle the more sensitive issue. This man moves through life like an actor on a stage. Let's see what a dose of reality does.*

"During the course of that enlightening conversation, what did your wife tell you about her affair . . . the affair she had with Neal Henderson?"

The older man's body stiffened. His lips grew thinner, but he didn't avert his eyes.

"No need for a sarcastic tone, Detective." He uncrossed his legs and sat even straighter. "She related the whole sordid story in a torrent of tears and self-recrimination. It wasn't necessary."

"You didn't care?" Tom sounded incredulous.

"It wasn't because I didn't care, but I'd known about the affair for some time. I decided to let it run its course. I never doubted she'd end it. He was an unprincipled money grubber. No one she could seriously care for.

To be truthful, I could never understand why my friend, Don Carson, turned his business over to the young man the way he did. I guess it had something to do with the boys growing up together, but Henderson never held a candle to Don's son."

"I've heard the same opinion expressed by others."

"Because it's true."

"Let's go back to your knowledge of your wife's affair." Tom knew the answers to his next questions were key to his investigation. "How did you find out and when?"

Art Patton sighed deeply. The man's acting skills served him well, but he couldn't hide the pain in his voice. "Max told me. It was one of the most difficult things he's ever done, but he felt I should know. He knew, of course, because he drove her to several rendezvous during their little dalliance."

Tom noted the man's choice of words in describing his wife's affair tended to depict it as something of small concern. *Was his wife's affair of so little import to his pride? If he still loved this woman deeply as he proclaimed, how much pain had Henderson brought into his life? Enough to give him cause for murder?*

He repeated his second question. "When did you learn of the affair?"

"Shortly before his demise," the actor admitted, "but it doesn't mean the events are interlinked."

"How did you respond to the news Max gave you?"

"I could see how badly the affair might end for Margaret in terms of her position with the City and her reputation in town. I decided to try to meet with him, to talk some sense into him."

"Shouldn't that conversation have been with your wife?"

"The last thing I wanted was for Margaret to think I was spying on her, or that Max was. She would never have felt comfortable around either of us again. But I also realized she was still too emotionally attached or she would have ended it herself."

"And what about Neal? What made you think he wasn't too emotionally attached to listen to you, especially with you being the indignant husband?"

Art Patton blanched. For the first time, he showed signs of how distasteful the conversation was for him. Tom could hardly imagine how distasteful dealing with Neal Henderson must have been.

"Men like Neal Henderson always have a price, Detective. I had no doubt I could offer him adequate inducement."

"Did your meeting happen to take place the night he was murdered?"

The actor shifted uneasily in his chair, looking at the folded hands in his lap.

"In fact, I did speak to Neal Henderson the night of his death. But it was a brief exchange. The conversation we were meant to have never took place."

Tom pulled out his notebook. His tone, as well as the tone of the entire conversation, had taken a three-hundred-and-sixty-degree turn.

"Please tell me exactly what happened between you and Mr. Henderson the night of his murder."

"I called his office. I told his assistant I wanted to speak with him on one of his investment projects in which I had interest. Once I had him on the phone, I informed him what I wanted to speak to him about was of a personal nature. He understood immediately."

"How did he respond to your request?"

"He was rude but agreed to see me. He said he had something to take care of that evening but would meet me afterward in the lounge of the hotel next to the Pier on the Boardwalk."

"Did he indicate a time?"

"He said he would be finished with the first matter by nine-thirty and we could meet shortly after."

Tom assumed the dead man's logic for the night in question. *His meet with the brothers was scheduled for nine o'clock. He knew he could see Patton shortly after his payoff to them because of the proximity of the hotel to the parking lot at the Pier.*

"What happened next?"

"I had Max drive me to the Pier. Margaret was out of town giving a speech at some convention or other so Max was free with the car. When we got to the lot, I told Max to park and wait for me. On my way to the hotel, I heard someone speaking loudly as if on a cell phone. I recognized the voice; it was the voice of the man I had come to see."

"Did you continue to the meeting place?"

"No." The older man's voice began to tremble. "No, in the next instant, I made one of the biggest mistakes of my life, one I deeply regret."

Tom's pulse raced with the excitement of obtaining a confession. He tried to keep his voice calm: "What did you do, Mr. Patton?"

"Not thinking clearly, I walked toward the voice. Seeing he was alone, I began spewing out the speech I had rehearsed.

191

Before I had spoken more than a few words, he turned on me. He looked furious, almost like one possessed. It was quite frightening, actually. He screamed for me to leave, he would see me at our arranged time and place. With that, he turned his back on me like I didn't exist.

My fright turned to a cold, steely anger. This man who had defiled my marriage was now unwilling to even acknowledge me. A fury welled inside me unlike anything I've experienced. I grabbed the closest rock within reach, walked up behind him, and took a swipe at the back of his head. He fell onto his knees, then collapsed on the sand. I threw the rock into the ocean and walked back to my car."

"Did you give any thought to going back to help the man?"

"I never imagined the blow I struck was enough to do more than give him a bad headache. I'm not a strong man; it was hardly more than a glancing blow. I couldn't believe it when I heard the news the next morning he was dead."

"The knock on the head was not the cause of death. The cause of death was strangulation. You hadn't killed Neal Henderson."

"I realized that when the coroner's report was finally released indicating the cause of death as strangulation. I'll admit my relief was immense though I was certain the whole time my blow could not have been deadly."

"Once you knew your blow hadn't killed him, what stopped you from giving the police the information about your encounter the night of his death?"

The actor pulled a handkerchief from his pocket and dabbed at his lips. "At that point, I considered going to the police to disclose everything that had taken place but I still had one reservation."

"Which was?"

192

"I knew my wife couldn't have been involved with the act itself, but I'm ashamed to admit I wondered if she might have put someone up to getting rid of him."

"You suspected her of hiring someone to kill Neal Henderson?"

"I realized almost at once how ridiculous the notion was but when you went to City Hall to question her, I worried you had the same suspicion. It was actually a relief when you called to see me. I was ready to tell the truth to ensure no suspicion fell on my wife." He paused, clasping his hands. "Believe what you will, Detective, but if I had seriously believed my blow to the head had been the actual cause of the man's death, I would have come forward sooner."

Tom's skepticism showed in his squinted eyes. "Let's get back to what happened that night. Did Max drive you straight home after your confrontation with Neal?"

"Actually, no. I was shaken by the ordeal, especially the violent reaction I'd had to Neal shunning me the way he did. I'm not a violent man. To the contrary, the only thing I've ever been accused of is being too nice, of being a pushover.

At any rate, Max noticed the state I was in. I mumbled something to him about having done something terrible without getting into specifics. He suggested I go to the hotel and have a brandy to settle my nerves before my meeting. I told him there would be no meeting, but a brandy sounded like a good idea.

He walked me to the hotel and returned to the car to wait for me. The brandy settled my nerves considerably. Max and I returned home without further incident."

"How long were you at the hotel by yourself?"

"As long as it takes to order and drink cognac. There were few people in the lounge so I was waited on almost immediately."

"How did Max act when you returned?"

"I hadn't thought about it. Why are you asking?"

Tom remained silent letting his question take hold. The actor's entire body collapsed against his chair. Taking several moments to recover, he asked shakily: "What are you suggesting, Detective? What has Max done?"

Chapter Twenty-One

Both men leaped to their feet.

"Max's Place," Art Patton cried.

Without understanding the reference, Tom knew where to look for the driver. They raced through the archway toward the guest house nearly knocking over the housekeeper sweeping the veranda. Running past the fountain in the courtyard next to the main building, Tom cursed. The limousine was no longer parked in the driveway. A quick peek through the windows of the guest house confirmed his fear: the man he was looking for was no longer on the premises.

"Get in, Mr. Patton," Tom yelled, pointing to his car. He issued additional instructions as they clicked their seat belts in place. "Call Max." The authoritative inflection in the Detective's voice left no room for hesitation. "Now."

The older man's hands trembled as he lifted his cell phone in front of him where they could both hear the conversation. "Max, it's Art. Where are you?"

"Your wife called. Her luncheon is finished. She's back in her office."

"Why are you going to pick her up now? She won't be through working for several hours."

"She said she has one more meeting, and then she wants to come home. Something about giving Rosa the night off and cooking dinner for you herself tonight."

Tom hastily jotted something on his notepad and held it in front of Art. He didn't want Max to overhear him giving instructions.

"Wait there for me, Max. I'm on my way. I need to see my wife about something. I'll see you shortly." He disconnected without waiting for a response.

"Is that what you wanted, Detective?"

"Perfect. No chance for him to ask how you're getting to town without the car. He saw me going into your house. I don't want him to think you're with me."

Art shook his head and looked out the window. "I'm afraid you could be underestimating him."

Tom grabbed his ringing cell from the dashboard. Reading caller ID, he tried to avoid sounding curt. "Hey, Paul. I'm right in the middle of something."

"No problem. I'll make this brief. I just picked up a voice message from Lea. She's all excited. Says Councilwoman Patton called her this afternoon about a change in plans. Lea's bid has been accepted after all. She's getting the job for the City. I know she'll want to celebrate tonight. Can you join us?"

"Where's Lea, Paul?" Tom demanded.

"Now? When she left the message, she was on her way to City Hall to see the Councilwoman." Paul heard the tension in his friend's voice. "What's wrong?"

"It's Max. He's on his way to Mrs. Patton's office."

Paul could feel his heart pounding as he repeated. "It's Max? What do you mean, it's Max?"

"Max killed Neal Henderson."

The only sound in the car was vehicles whizzing by on the freeway. There was no response on the speaker phone.

"Paul?"

"Is Lea in danger?"

Tom hoped his voice conveyed more confidence than he felt. "I have another car on the way. We have the situation under control. No one's going to get hurt."

"I'm going to City Hall."

"You can't help, Paul. You could make things worse," Tom warned.

"Don't tell me not to get involved if my wife could be in danger." The line went dead.

196

$$* * *$$

Arriving for her appointment with Margaret Patton, Lea was caught off guard when the secretary asked Lea to bring her dog into the office.

Are repercussions in store for our aggressive approach during our last encounter? Lea wondered.

The Assistant smiled reassuringly, "I believe the Councilwoman wants to make amends for the way you and your dog were received."

Seeing the skepticism in Lea's face, she continued: "She really does like dogs, you know. Not as much as her husband, of course, but she told me that even with all the excitement and flying fur last time you met, she could see what a beautiful animal you have. She'd like to make your dog's acquaintance under friendlier conditions."

Lea laughed, relieved. "Of course, but I thought dogs weren't allowed inside government offices."

"Bring her in the back way from the parking lot. She won't be noticed. Besides," the woman added, winking, "no one questions the Councilwoman."

Walking in from the parking lot, Lea gave Gracie firm instructions about not repeating her previous behavior, a rebuke which proved to be unnecessary. She held her breath as the Councilwoman met them at the door, kneeling in front of the dog and offering to shake hands. Gracie obliged by raising a paw.

When the diminutive woman stood and returned to her chair, Gracie followed obediently, curling comfortably at her feet under the oversized desk.

I'll never understand my dogs. Gracie was upset yesterday but obviously, not by this woman.

Lea was further confounded by the woman's opening remark. "You made quite an impression chasing me down in front of City Hall the way you did."

197

Experiencing an uncomfortable heat sensation crawling up her neck, she mumbled: "I'm so embarrassed to have run after you that way, but Gracie was pulling me and . . ."

"It's quite alright, Lea. It wasn't your flying hair that made the impression. It was what you said. You challenged my reason for not awarding you the contract."

Lea's head jerked back. "You mean I was right?"

"I'm not willing to admit that yet, even to myself, but it was close enough to the truth to cause me to examine my other recent actions. I've had a change of heart in more than one area."

Lea remained silent, sensing the Councilwoman wanted to continue uninterrupted.

"A Detective came to see me shortly after you and I had our confrontation. The interview was brutal enough to knock some sense into me. It made me step back to look at myself. I didn't much like what I saw."

She brushed a hand in front of her face. "But you aren't interested in hearing about my epiphany. All you need to know is your bid has been accepted. Once I set aside my personal feelings, I had to admit your proposal was by far the best we received."

Lea stopped holding her breath and allowed a smile to spread across her face. "I hardly know what to say besides thank you very much."

"You deserve the project, Lea. I look forward to working with you on it."

As both women rose to shake hands, the door was flung open and Max rushed into the office.

"Max. What in the world . . ."

Lea hardly recognized the man who came running around the desk to grab the Councilwoman. Without the chauffeur's hat he typically wore, his bald pate gleamed. His shirt was soaked with perspiration. His eyes were a mesmerizing mix of madness and calm determination.

The secretary came rushing through the door, freezing the moment she saw Max standing behind her employer, pinning the woman's arms to her sides.

"Shut the door and sit down," he ordered.

Rosemary hesitated, looking to her boss for confirmation.

"Do as he says. At the moment, he's literally got the upper hand." Regaining her authoritarian tone of voice, she looked over her shoulder and demanded, "What's the meaning of this, Max?"

Before Rosemary could close the door as the man had instructed, Tom and Art came storming through it. An emotion flashed across Max's face when he saw his employer, but Lea couldn't define what he was feeling.

Instead of trying to approach his driver directly, Art slipped onto the couch to the side of the desk, asking gently. "Max. My dear, dear Max. What are you doing, my good fellow?"

The response was formal and respectful. "I'm sorry, sir. Extreme actions have been called for, I'm afraid. I knew when you called you were with the Detective. You two have figured it out, haven't you?"

Art had never lied to his bodyguard in all their years together. He wasn't about to start now.

"I'm sorry to say, yes. Sorry for your sake, my dear man."

"Art," his wife implored, "will you please tell me what you two are talking about?"

The two men stared at each other across the silent room, but no response was forthcoming.

Tom provided the answer. "Max killed Neal Henderson."

The beefy man's reaction to the Detective's words was instinctively defensive as though he were under attack. Every muscle in his body flexed. His jaw clenched. He tightened his grip, causing the Councilwoman to wince.

In that tense instant, the border collie flew out from under the desk catapulting her body like a missile. Thrown off balance, Max stumbled backward allowing Tom to throw a punch on target enough to flatten the man. In a flash, Gracie was on top of him, baring her teeth and growling.

"Thanks, girl, I'll take it from here." Tom quickly pulled handcuffs from his belt, attaching them to the man's wrists. Punching a number in his cell phone, the Detective gave instructions for the squad car dispatched earlier to City Hall.

Everyone in the room struggled to grasp what had taken place in front of them.

Art embraced his wife. She leaned on him, letting him walk her over to the couch where they sat down and held each other. "I can't believe it, Art. I can't believe Max killed someone. Why did he do it?"

Everyone turned to the actor. What they saw was no act. Pain showed clearly in every feature on his face.

Knowing the man was overcome with emotion, the Detective provided an answer. There was more sadness in Tom's voice than harshness. "Probably because Neal Henderson hurt and disrespected the man he's looked up to his entire life."

His words were like a punch in the stomach to Max. The fight in him was clearly gone. His shoulders sagged. His eyes glistened with tears.

"It's all gone wrong, sir," he moaned, looking at his lifelong benefactor. "I don't know how it's all gone so terribly wrong."

Everyone in the room was startled to see the powerful man's body suddenly wracked by sobs.

Margaret Patton was the first to grasp the full meaning of Tom's explanation. "Oh, no. He did it because of the pain caused by my affair."

Her husband turned to face her, taking her hand in his own. "Don't blame yourself. I was cast in the worst role of my life, that of a cuckold. But it was my own foolish mistake to arrange to speak with Neal myself. I found his behavior toward me embarrassingly demeaning. In a moment of anger, I hit him with a rock.

Apparently, while I was recovering from my appalling emotional display, Max went to see the horrible thing I told him I'd done. Looking out for me, as he's always done." He turned around. "Is that how it happened, Max?"

"Yes, sir." Max put his elbows on his knees and buried his head in his hands. "He wasn't conscious when I found him under the Pier, but I could see the wound you inflicted wasn't serious. Standing over him, all the hatred I'd been feeling toward your wife welled up inside me. She's never treated me as an equal as you always have; she's never been kind. You deserved better, too, sir. You've always deserved better. When I realized she was carrying on with the likes of that upstart, I couldn't stand what it might do to you."

Art stood over the broken man, putting an arm on his shoulder. "But, Max, I've always been happy with Margaret. You've never understood our relationship, I know, but it works for us. I can see now I should have shared my feelings about her with you. Maybe then you would have known I was alright. My honor didn't need defending. My heart was never broken." His voice choked. "Until now."

Tom was the first to recover from the startling revelations. "One point I'd like to clarify, Max. Were you the one who broke into Neal's condominium?"

Max sighed, looking at his employer. "I was afraid he might have something incriminating against Madam. I was sure he wouldn't hesitate to blackmail one or both of you. All I found was a picture of her talking to him at the fundraiser. It wasn't much, but I didn't want him to have any proof of their carrying on."

Tom didn't mention the picture Max hadn't found; the one that could, indeed, have been used for blackmail.

An officer appeared at the doorway. Tom helped Max to his feet and the officer marched him out.

"I'll do everything I can for you, Max," Art promised as they passed.

The Pattons were the first to take their leave. Art reminded his wife they were without a driver. She laughed: "Don't worry, Honey. I can drive that big, black limousine. Next week, we're trading it in for something more practical. With more cargo room to take the dogs to their shows. Something I can see out of, without all that darn window tinting. Right now, I'm taking you home to cook up the best meal you've never had from me."

He hooked his arm in hers, smiling. A gleam was returning to his eyes.

"I can't thank you yet, Detective," he told Tom. "The heartbreak of the outcome is still too fresh. Someday, I'll be able to appreciate how well you've done your job. When that time comes, I hope to find a way to repay you."

"But not by bribery," his wife was quick to add, bringing them all some much-needed laughter. "That reminds me . . . all kinds of interesting things have been happening since you three started gracing City Hall with your presence."

"What are you referring to?" Paul asked.

"Charles White resigned today. Didn't give much reason other than his wife wanting to move closer to their grandchildren. Took everyone by surprise. Except me, maybe." The corners of her mouth lifted in a small smile as she looked at Tom. "You wouldn't know anything about that, would you, Detective?"

Tom shrugged his shoulders, looking in turn toward Paul. "I'm as surprised as anyone. I have no idea what precipitated his resignation."

The Councilwoman pressed Lea's hand as she and her husband turned to leave. "My special thanks to you, Lea, for bringing me to my senses in time for me to have a second chance at getting things right. You and I will talk soon."

The friends watched the couple walk toward their limousine as a setting sun of burning red and orange began slowly disappearing into the ocean.

A janitor walked in, then quickly backed out. "Sorry, I thought the Councilwoman was done for the day."

The threesome looked at each other, nodding. Lea swept her arm in front of her. "Come on in. We're all done for the day."

Paul grinned. "We've each got our own car. The last one to the Crab Shack buys drinks."

As they raced down the hallway, Lea asked, "Should I . . ."

The two men shouted in unison. "Yes . . . call Maddy."

Book Two of the Sister Sleuths Mystery Series

A well-plotted mystery with a theatre setting that rings authentic, a smart cast of characters, and plenty of twists and turns to keep you guessing.

To My Readers,

Thank you so much for joining Lea and Maddy . . . and the dogs . . . in their sleuthing adventures.

If you enjoyed your time spent with them, would you please consider posting a review? Reviews are very helpful to other readers and are greatly appreciated.

If you have questions or comments, I can be reached at raynamorgan2@gmail.com and would love to hear from you.

Until their next adventure,
Rayna

Made in the USA
Lexington, KY
23 November 2016